THE PALE OF SETTLEMENT

winner of the flannery o'connor award for short fiction

the university of georgia press ~ athens and london

STORIES BY

MARGOT SINGER

THE PALE OF
SETTLEMENT

Published by the University of Georgia Press

Athens, Georgia 30602

© 2007 by Margot Singer

Designed by Mindy Basinger Hill

Set in 11/15 pt Filosofia

The paper in this book meets the guidelines for
permanence and durability of the Committee on
Production Guidelines for Book Longevity of the
Council on Library Resources.

Printed in the United States of America

11 10 09 08 07 c 5 4 3 2 1

Library of Congress Cataloging-in-Publication Data

Singer, Margot.

The Pale of Settlement : stories / Margot Singer.

    p. cm. — (The Flannery O'Connor Award for Short Fiction)

ISBN-13: 978-0-8203-3000-6 (alk. paper)

ISBN-10: 0-8203-3000-0 (alk. paper)

1. Jews—Identity—Fiction. 2. Jewish diaspora—Fiction. I. Title.

PS3619.I572447 2007

813'.6—dc22   2007015079

British Library Cataloging-in-Publication Data available

FOR MY PARENTS

Through the window that is not there, we see our children

searching the old ruin for toys they lost yesterday

and turning up broken clay jars from centuries ago.

The chasm between generations fills up with dust and sand,

human bones, animal bones, a multitude of broken vessels.

Broken jars speak the truth. A new jar is the lie of beauty.

YEHUDA AMICHAI ~ from "Summer and the Far End of Prophesy"

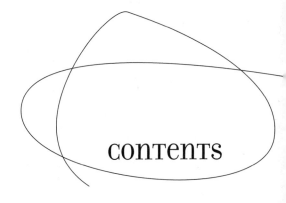

contents

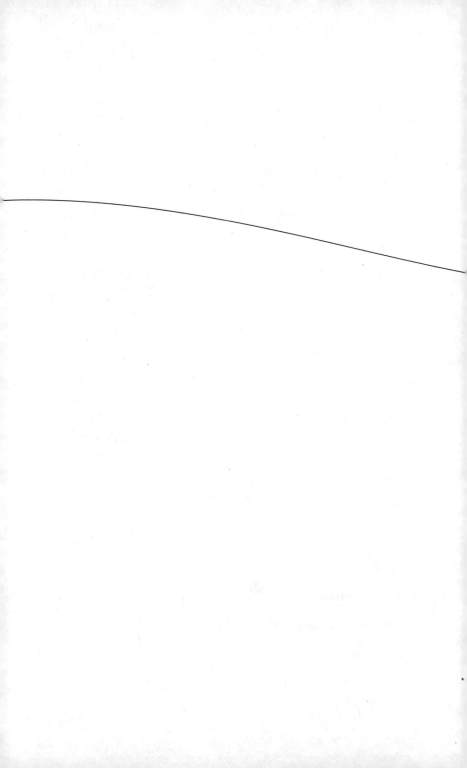

ACKNOWLEDGMENTS

Many of the stories in this collection first appeared in journals (some in slightly different form): "Helicopter Days" in *Ascent*; "Reunification" in *Agni*; "Lila's Story" in *Shenandoah*; "As Dawn Splits" (the first section of "Deir Yassin") in the *Mid-American Review*; "Borderland" in the *Gettysburg Review*; "Deir Yassin" and "Hazor" in the *Western Humanities Review*; "Body Count" in *Prairie Schooner*; and "The Pale of Settlement" in the *North American Review*.

The lines from Hannah Senesh's poem "Now" appear with the permission of Stuart Matlins, publisher, Jewish Lights Publishing.

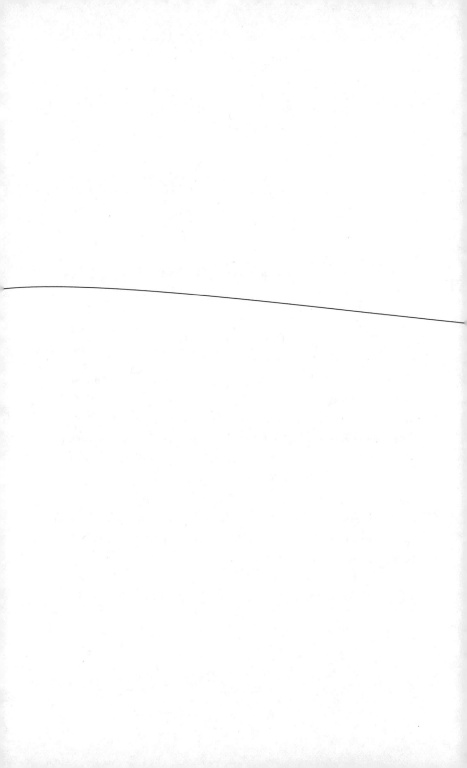

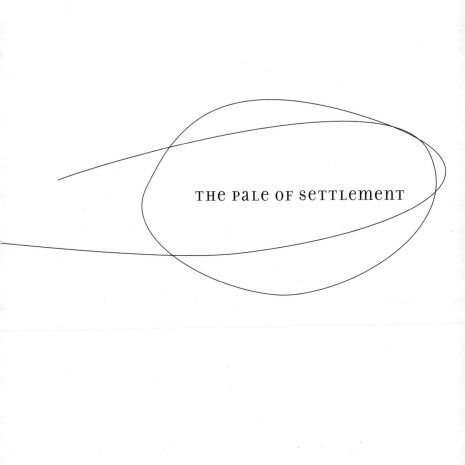

THE PALE OF SETTLEMENT

Love is a simultaneous firing of two spirits
engaged in the autonomous act of growing
up. And the sensation is of something having
noiselessly exploded inside each of them.
LAWRENCE DURRELL, *Justine*

Helicopter Days

The bomb went off downtown, near the entrance to the Haifa Carmelit subway, at 5:27 on a Friday morning in late June. It blew up a white Fiat and shattered the plate glass windows of the Bank Hapoalim branch across the intersection. It exploded a streetlight, two signposts, and part of the stone wall bordering the sidewalk on the subway side of the street. The lower branches of a eucalyptus tree were burned clear of leaves, and the trunk was singed with streaks of black, like a primitive drawing. The pavement was covered with bits of twisted metal and broken stone.

The dawning light was gray as glass. Along the beaches, less than a kilometer away, waves folded over on the sand. Halfway up Mount Carmel, a muezzin called the faithful to prayer from a loudspeaker mounted on a minaret. In the cypresses that lined the steep slope of the Baha'i gardens, below the temple's golden dome, jays woke and began to chatter, agitating the branches of the trees. Near the top of the Carmel, from the couch in her father's old room where

1

she slept behind green *trissim* folded down against the light, Susan did not hear the explosion on the Hadar. Other sounds came to her as if through water: the clink of cutlery, a barking dog, the murmur of a radio. The Voice of Israel reported in its nine o'clock broadcast that no one had been injured in the blast. Other than a disruption to traffic, everything was functioning as normal. Only a few commuters, stepping out of the Carmelit station into the daylight, noticed the smell of burned rubber, the toppled poles, the unswept bits of glass.

During that summer of the 1982 war in Lebanon, nothing seemed dangerous the way Susan had imagined it would. That summer, the first time Susan had come to Israel on her own, she walked with her grandmother as usual to the corner *makolet* to buy plastic sacks of milk and loaves of bread; on the *merkaz*, people sat outside in the cafés, drinking coffee and smoking, as they always did. There were soldiers about, kids her age, hitchhiking at bus stops or by the beach, the boys with M16s slung over their shoulders, the girls in khaki skirts and caps, but that, too, was nothing new. When Susan's parents telephoned from New York, she assured them everything was fine. Still, there was a tension in the air, like the faint buzz of high-voltage power lines: a sense of the borders just there, around that headland, over those hills. The narrowness of the land.

From her grandparents' terrace, Susan could see the army helicopters landing on the roof of Rambam hospital. On some days, bad days, she counted ten or fifteen at a time, pulsing low along the horizon on their way in, arcing high out over the bay on their return to the north. Lebanon was barely twenty miles away, less than the distance from Susan's parents' apartment in Riverdale to

the bottom of Staten Island. Even though she couldn't understand most of the newscaster's words, Susan watched the news each evening on TV, footage of Israeli soldiers waving to their families back home, women in bikinis sunbathing on the beaches near Beirut, rows of Mercedes parked along the palm tree–lined boulevards. Look at that, Susan's aunt said, they don't care about the war at all! But hadn't Susan gone to the beach herself that very day? A story ran in the *Jerusalem Post* claiming that a photograph of an armless Lebanese orphan wounded by Israeli shelling was, in fact, a healthy Druze child with limbs and parents both intact. Susan studied the grainy photograph that showed a baby swaddled in a blanket in the arms of a Red Cross nurse. It was impossible to tell.

Her friends back in New York didn't consider Israel a safe place. Don't things blow up over there all the time? they said. Once, as a little girl, Susan had reached for an empty plastic jug lying on the ground, and her grandmother had slapped her, hard, on the hand. Never, ever touch anything you find on the street! her grandmother scolded. You never know what could be a bomb! But the truth was Susan had never encountered anything remotely dangerous there. Israel was the place her parents and all her relatives were from. It was almost home.

Susan's cousin Gavi was in the army, stationed near the Syrian border in the Golan Heights. Most weeks, he came home on Friday night for Shabbat, just as if he had a regular job. He sprawled on the couch, his army boots unlaced and shirt unbuttoned, watching *Dallas* reruns on TV. Susan wanted to know what it was like along the front. She wanted details: the sound of shelling, the soldiers wounded or dead.

No, Gavi said, shaking his head and making the tsk-tsk sound

Israelis always made when you said something they considered stupid. It's not like that at all. Mostly we just sit around with nothing much to do.

Susan kept a photograph of Gavi pinned to the bulletin board above her desk back at college. He stood tall and broad shouldered in his uniform, backed by a picture-postcard view of Haifa bay. Friends who came by Susan's room sometimes asked if he was her boyfriend, and sometimes she said yes, just for fun.

They were paired from birth, Susan and Gavi, her mother and her aunt due on the same day, although in the end she was a few weeks early and he a few days late, making her a Taurus and him a Gemini, her an earth sign, him air. They all matched, she and Gavi, her two younger brothers and his. Their grandparents took annual summer photographs of the six cousins posed on the living room couch, propped-up babies in the early shots, awkward adolescents in the more recent ones, with freckles and shiny orthodontic grins. The framed photographs hung in the cluster of family pictures that lined the hallway outside her grandparents' bedroom, and Susan always found herself studying them when she first arrived in Israel, wondering what they would look like when they were all grown up.

As children, she and Gavi played games in two languages, with made-up words. Gavi always made her shriek and then laughed when the grown-ups scolded her for making too much noise. She challenged him to races, which he invariably won. For a time, they wrote letters to each other, hers in bad Hebrew, his in bad English, sometimes in a mixture of both. She felt close to him, closer than seemed likely given their few summer weeks together every year,

given the language barrier, but each summer they just picked up where they'd left off as if no time had passed at all.

Gavi says he'd like a girlfriend just like you, Susan's grandmother told her, that summer of the Lebanon war, the summer they were nineteen. It gave her a twinge to hear that, almost like love.

That summer, at the end of June, Gavi got a few days leave and borrowed a truck from his unit and they drove south together, past Tel Aviv and Ashdod and Ashkelon to where the land flattened out and dissolved into ochre sand. Susan rolled down the window and let the wind whip through her hair. There on the front seat next to Gavi, she felt a tingling excitement in her veins and wondered if this was how it would feel to travel with a boyfriend of her own. In the late afternoon, Gavi turned off the coastal highway onto a narrow road that ran through a plain of drifted sand crisscrossed with rows of tufted grass and irrigation ducts, clusters of Arab houses roofed with corrugated tin, chickens pecking in the dust. Gavi drove to where the road curved along the sea and pulled over on the verge. There was an army base just up the road, he said, that he'd spent time at during basic training, and he'd promised himself that he'd come back. The base was surrounded by settlements belonging to ultra-Orthodox Jews. There had been three settlements a year ago; there were seven now. Susan knew they had to be very close to, or in, the Gaza Strip. Her aunt and uncle had said specifically to stay away from there.

Are you sure it's safe? she said.

Gavi frowned and made the tsk-tsk sound. It's okay, he said.

They climbed out of the truck and pushed through scrub grass to the beach. Rows of separate palm-frond huts for the religious men and women lined the shore. Waves hissed along the untracked sand. The sea was a living, electric blue.

After they had swum and eaten the cheese and hummus and pita bread her aunt had packed, they sat next to each other on the sand and watched the sun sink into the sea. Darkness dropped quickly here and, away from the city lights, it felt dense as fog. They passed a cigarette back and forth, although neither of them really smoked, the orange tip fading in and out like a tiny flare. Gavi leaned back on his elbows and pointed out the constellations—Cepheus, Andromeda, Cassiopeia—tracing their outlines with his hand.

Did you know that by the time the light from those stars reaches our eyes, he said, the stars might no longer exist?

Perhaps there's just a big black canopy up there, Susan said, lit with golden lamps. She meant it as a joke, an allusion to romantic poetry, but as she spoke, the image suddenly seemed more likely than what she knew from high school physics about spectrography and Doppler shifts and black holes deep in space. Maybe, she said, none of it is real.

She lay on her back, letting her arm roll outward to touch Gavi's. The stars didn't seem to be the same stars she remembered from New York. As she gazed upward, they fell toward her like fireflies.

Look how beautiful it is, Gavi said, not moving his arm away. These stars, this sky.

By the time Susan finished college, the pattern of annual summer visits to Israel with her parents and brothers had fallen off for good. Susan flew to Israel by herself to celebrate her grandfather's eighty-seventh birthday over her spring break from journalism school. She sat on the couch in her grandparents' living room, sipping champagne, and tried to memorize it all: the fraying Oriental carpet, the tile floor, the discordant mingling of German and English and Hebrew speech, the humidity, the scent of pine.

Sharona, Gavi's girlfriend, sat down next to her on the couch. Sharona was a forthright girl with close-set eyes and plump, soft hands; she wore her hair in a spiky, blond-streaked shag. She spoke English fluently, much better than anyone in Susan's Israeli family. Susan didn't think she and Sharona were much alike at all.

So, when are you going to come to live in Israel, make aliyah? Sharona asked.

I don't know, one of these days, Susan said. She didn't imagine that her boyfriend, who favored preppy button-downs and Levi's cords, would move to Israel with her. What American would? Even her parents would not be pleased. Even they had left and not come back.

Susan's uncle came in carrying a reel-to-reel projector and several metal canisters of film. Movie time! he said. Susan's grandfather had shot the sixteen-millimeter film in the 1920s and '30s, before the war, before they came to Palestine. Susan squeezed closer to Sharona to make room for her grandparents on the couch, and Gavi dimmed the lights. Her grandmother perched upright on the arm of the couch, her knobby hands clasped in her lap. No one had seen the films in years. The light flickered on the wall and then there was her grandmother, a cloche tipped at an angle over her bobbed hair, posing by a motor car parked on a hairpin curve along a Swiss mountain road. There were her grandparents skiing in the Alps, in woolen knickers and jackets, with bamboo poles and wooden skis. There was a baby, all rolls of fat, crawling naked on the grass. Her grandfather said something in German and everybody laughed. What do you think of your Daddy? Susan's uncle translated. The baby pulled up on a chair and let out an arc of pee.

He was a terrible boy, her grandfather said, and again everybody laughed.

That's the garden of my parents' house, Susan's grandmother said, pressing a tissue to her eyes. It was very beautiful there.

The next day, Gavi invited Susan to go to the Galilee to see the wildflowers. They squeezed into the front seat of Gavi's truck, Sharona in the middle and Gavi and Susan on either side. It was a gusty March day; Susan had never been in Israel when there were clouds in the sky, when the light lacked the blunt white glare of heat. They hiked up Mount Tabor; in the hazy distance, Susan could see Nazareth, the green-brown hills of the West Bank. She tried to imagine the early Israelites Devorah and Barak standing on this spot three thousand years ago, preparing to launch their assault on Canaanite Hazor. Susan took out her camera and shot a roll of Gavi and Sharona kneeling among the anemones and irises in the blowing grass. She squinted at them through the Nikon's telephoto lens, at their close-up smiles and entwined hands, and felt envy rise within her like a blush.

Susan's flight back to New York was delayed for five hours due to an air-traffic controllers' strike in Paris. She found out when the taxi dropped her off at Ben Gurion at midnight, and there was nothing to do but wait. She sat on a plastic chair outside security and tried to read. A group of teenagers were curled like caterpillars in sleeping bags along the wall, and she fought the urge to lie down next to them and sleep. Behind her, male and female soldiers stood alongside tables, rummaging through suitcases, asking questions. Where in Israel have you been? Did you pack your bags yourself? Did anyone give you something to carry for them? A fair-haired girl, a kibbutz volunteer from Scandinavia or Germany, Susan guessed, was crying as a soldier pulled clothes and underwear out of her backpack. No one ever searched Susan's bags.

When she next looked up from her book, Gavi was standing right there, in a group of people waiting to check in to a flight to Greece, no more than a few yards away. He was staring out above her head, or right through her, and she began to wave to him, but there was something so strange about his expression that she felt a sudden stab of uncertainty and lowered her arm again. Was it Gavi? They'd had dinner together not six hours before, kissed each other good-bye—he'd said nothing about a trip. Could there be some mistake? But it was Gavi—it had to be.

She put down her book and stood up, walked over to where he stood. She was almost in front of him before he let his eyes meet hers, raising one hand in a gesture that didn't quite mean surrender, but wasn't exactly a wave. He was wearing glasses and his eyes looked tired and red.

Gavi? she said.

Please, he said. Don't tell anyone you've seen me.

What are you doing here?

I'm just going on a trip to Crete, together with some friends, only for two days. It's the, how do you say, not the solstice—

The equinox?

Yes—it's very nice. We make some music together, talk, look at the sky. You know. But the parents, Sharona, they don't understand—please.

Susan felt a hollow space behind her ribs. Of course I won't say anything, she said. You know you can trust me.

Gavi glanced back at two men who were watching him from their place in line. They had army buzz cuts just like Gavi's, tidy clothes—clean-cut types. Gavi nodded to them, picked up his bag.

I have to go, he said. This time he didn't kiss her, just gave a little wave good-bye.

Bye, she said.

And what could be so bad about a stargazing trip to Crete? But the whole flight home, she sat with an anxious feeling creeping about inside her chest, as if somehow she'd become an accomplice to a crime.

Susan said nothing to anyone about Gavi's trip to Greece, but by the time she got home to her apartment in New York, the light on her answering machine was already blinking with the news.

Susan called her parents back. Out the window, the afternoon sun glinted off a helicopter flying south along the Hudson's New Jersey shore.

It's a terrible thing, her father said. I don't know what meshugas has got into that boy's head.

Just because he's going to Crete for a couple of days, he's crazy? Susan said.

Everyone is terribly upset! her father said. Sharona has given him an ultimatum—the group or her, he has to choose. He promised her he wouldn't go, and then he sneaks away behind everybody's back.

What group? Susan said, wondering why Gavi hadn't told her anything about this. She pictured waves folding over on Aegean sand, the sound of a guitar, a black sky cupped with stars.

When we were young, her father said, things were different in Israel. Life had meaning then. It's not the same anymore.

It's the pressure, Susan's mother said, joining in from an extension in the other room. It's too much, really, for anyone to bear.

Her father made the tsk-tsk sound with his tongue. He said, The boy's got his head stuck in the clouds.

A few days later, when Susan got her film developed from the trip, she found the photograph her uncle had taken of the whole family, that last evening after dinner, before she left for the airport. She was sitting on her grandparents' couch, leaning in toward Sharona and her younger cousins, smiling wide. Gavi was standing next to her, his hands pushed into the pockets of his jeans. What she noticed now was his eyes, which were puffy and a little blurred, as if you were looking up at them through the bottom of a glass.

A few weeks later, Susan got a call from an Israeli named Tal who was living in New York. He said Gavi had given him her phone number, and he asked her out. Gavi hadn't mentioned anyone named Tal to her, and Susan wondered why Gavi, who knew she had a serious boyfriend, would want to fix her up with someone else. Perhaps her aunt had put him up to it. Her aunt was determined to find her a suitable Jewish man. Susan didn't tell her boyfriend, but called Tal back and said, Okay.

Tal picked her up in his car, a rusty convertible lacking seatbelts and inside door handles, and took her to an Ethiopian restaurant up on 121st and Amsterdam, a part of the city Susan considered to be unsafe. They were the only white people in the place. Susan perched at the drumlike table, feeling tense and ill at ease, as Tal instructed her to touch her food only with her right hand and kept her glass filled with the cheap red wine he'd brought along in a paper bag. He had a thick ponytail and pale blue eyes like a husky's. He asked her constant questions as he mopped up the unidentifiable food, one-handed, with bits of spongy bread. How could she stand living in New York? Why wasn't she religious—didn't she consider herself a Jew? How could she want to be a journalist when they were all such parasites? Didn't she ever do anything sinful, just for fun?

This is what she didn't like about Israelis, Susan thought. She was not one of them at all. Her boyfriend would never antagonize her this way. She pictured the furrow that would appear between his eyes if he knew she was on a date with someone else and wished she hadn't come.

So do you know anything about this "group" that Gavi's joined? she asked Tal. What is it, some kind of a cult?

Already you have a negative attitude! he said. Do you think there is some difference between what you call "religion" and a cult?

Are you in it, too?

Tal took a swallow of wine and shrugged dismissively. He said, There are many things in this universe of ours that we cannot rationally understand.

After dinner, driving back downtown, Tal slowed and turned abruptly off the Harlem River Drive. He switched off the headlights and drove slowly, in darkness, along the riverfront path.

You do realize this is totally illegal, Susan said. Her heart was thumping high inside her throat. What was she doing here? What if Tal was, in fact, insane?

You worry too much, he said. Relax.

He stopped the car near the abutment of the George Washington Bridge, then came around to open her door. I'm going to show you something special, he said, peering in at her, as if she were the visitor in his city, not the other way around. He held out his hand and said, Come on.

Susan stepped out of the car and looked over the metal rail. The Hudson flowed below them black as asphalt in the dark. And then she saw it: the little lighthouse, perched on the stony embankment underneath the bridge, just like in the storybook she'd read as a child. She'd always known it was there but had never seen it up this close before. High above, the lights along the bridge span blinked like stars.

You can see it only from here, Tal said. Then he turned to Susan and pulled her to him. He pressed his tongue, warm and insistent, against hers. After a moment, she put her arms around his neck and wrapped her fingers in his thick rope of hair.

Looking back, Susan wondered how she could have missed the signs. Still, on the surface at least, everything seemed fine. She continued to take a week's vacation, most years, to visit her grandparents, who—there was no denying it—were slowly beginning to fail. Despite the flap over the trip to Crete, Gavi married Sharona, and Susan's younger cousins quickly followed suit. But rather than marrying her boyfriend, Susan broke up with him. Her grandparents sighed and gave their wedding rings to Gavi and Sharona instead. Her aunt redoubled her efforts to fix Susan up.

When Susan's grandfather died, one month after Saddam Hussein's 1990 invasion of Kuwait, Susan could not get off work in time to go to his funeral. Her parents phoned from Haifa afterward. Susan sat on her bed and watched the helicopters buzzing low along the Hudson as her parents described how the trees were already wrapped with death notices when they arrived, the Hebrew letters of her grandfather's name in black and white against the trunks of the Carmel pines. Then they told her how Sharona was there in the hospital as well, on the floor above the one Susan's grandfather was on, in labor with her first child. The baby was born within the hour of her grandfather's death. His eyes were a deep and radiant blue, just like his great-grandfather's. Everyone was saying that Susan's grandfather's soul had flown out of his body and into the baby boy's.

Then her parents began complaining, as they always did, about how much things had changed. There were Russians playing violins on every street corner; even supermarket signs were in Cyrillic now. There were three new high-rises on the *merkaz*; the view of the bay from Panorama Street was ruined. Everyone still smoked like chimneys. They drove like maniacs as well. There were more deaths from traffic accidents every year than in all the wars combined. Things can't go on like this, they said, the way they always did.

Susan turned on the news and watched the reports on Iraq's occupation of Kuwait, the experts' speculation about the likelihood of war. It didn't seem possible that so soon after the fall of the Berlin Wall and perestroika there should be such a threat to peace. This was nothing like the 1982 invasion of Lebanon; this time the Iraqi SCUDS were aimed directly at Haifa and Tel Aviv. She thought back to the Peace Now rally she'd gone to in a Tel Aviv park that summer of the Lebanon campaign, eight years before. The grounds were filled with tanks and mortars and other armaments captured from the Hezbollah in southern Lebanon. Those are the guns they want to kill us with, Gavi said as they wandered around the grim display, but none of it felt real. What she remembered best was afterward, sitting in an open-air café by the sea in Jaffa with Gavi and his friends—the balmy darkness, the chalky stone, the sound of the waves lapping at the shore. In the dark, she couldn't see Andromeda's rock, to which, according to the myth, the girl was lashed and left to drown. They'd smoked cigarettes and sipped small cups of Arabic coffee laced with cardamom and talked about the shelling of the Palestinian refugee camps in southern Lebanon, about Ariel Sharon, the Hezbollah, a friend who'd nearly lost an eye, the confusion of it all.

Would you ever come to live here? one of Gavi's friends had asked.

Here. *Ha'aretz*. The land.

Sure, maybe, someday, Susan said. She'd envied their purpose-fulness, the sense of meaning she felt their lives must have. Looking back, she wondered how she could have been so naive.

You have to be crazy to live here, one of them had said, tapping his finger on his temple. Meshuga! I'm getting the hell out of this nuthouse as soon as I can.

They'd all laughed, except Gavi.

I could never live anyplace else, he said.

When Susan went to Israel the next spring, her grandmother was alone. They sat together on the couch in the living room, sipping coffee and looking out onto the hazy vista of the bay. There were no helicopters today, only the long gray battleships of the U.S. Sixth Fleet. Susan had brought a tape recorder along, hoping to capture some of the stories of her grandparents' lives before it was too late, but now that she was there she wasn't sure she had the courage to take the machine out of her bag. It seemed, somehow, too much of an admission that her grandmother, too, would soon be dead. She studied the photographs lined up along the mantelpiece, portraits of her parents as newlyweds, of her grandfather in his officer's uniform from World War I, of herself and Gavi as babies playing at Khayat Beach, round and naked on the sand.

Her grandmother was telling her about the Iraqi scuds. One night, when the alarm sounded, she said, I was at your aunt and uncle's flat. We had to go into the bathroom, which was their sealed room. Imagine! There we were, sitting together on the edge of the bathtub, drinking champagne.

Champagne? Susan said. Weren't you supposed to have your gas masks on?

Yes, well, her grandmother said. There didn't seem much point.

Gavi came to visit their grandmother nearly every day. He pushed open the front door without bothering to ring the bell. He had filled out a bit since Susan had seen him last, and he'd let his hair grow out from its army buzz cut, but otherwise he seemed unchanged. Oh, my wonderful boy, their grandmother said, reaching her bent, arthritic arms around his neck and kissing him repeatedly on the cheek.

Gavi took Susan out for lunch to an overly bright health food restaurant with white plastic chairs and tables and bushy potted ferns. She didn't even try to speak Hebrew anymore, and his English was rusty from disuse. She watched him struggle to find the words and tried to keep her own vocabulary simple, her enunciation clear. He told her about the construction company he was working for, about a recent trip to Eilat. She told him about the series of stories she was writing about the homeless in New York and joked about the bad blind dates she'd recently been on. He didn't mention anything about his "group," and although she wondered if he was still involved with it, she didn't ask.

They were back in the car when Gavi turned to her and said, Would you come someplace with me?

It was a breezy day, too cool for the beach, the sky hung with banks of blurred gray clouds. Susan had nothing else to do, so she said, Sure.

Gavi drove to a neighborhood Susan had never been to before, down on the Hadar, near the Arab part of town. He parked in front of a concrete building Susan took at first to be a block of flats. Then she saw the sign and realized that it was a hotel. She tried to speak, but Gavi had already stepped around the car and was opening her door. She followed him into the building, and across the empty lobby, and then she watched as he exchanged some words with the clerk at the front desk and took his wallet out of his back pocket and pulled out several bills. The clerk unhooked a key from a pegboard on the wall and pointed to the elevator. Susan followed Gavi into the narrow space, fixed her eyes on the numbers lighting up overhead. The unsaid words dropped inside her as the elevator rose.

The room smelled of cigarette smoke and ammonia; it was dim and cold but clean. Gavi went to open the blinds and Susan sat on the edge of the bed and wondered who had been there before them, in this room rented out to men like Gavi by the hour or the day. And what kind of woman was she? There was a black telephone on the bedside table and a blinking digital clock. Here she was. Gavi sat down next to her. He laced his fingers together, examining his palms. Then he looked up and said, There's always been a special connection between us, don't you think?

Yes, Susan whispered, the word snagging in her throat. She thought of that evening on the beach in Gaza, the belated light of stars.

Then Gavi turned and put his arms around her and pulled her to him. She felt him release his breath, his body slackening against hers. He stayed there, holding her, his head against her shoulder, her cheek against his shirt, her hands resting on the broad slope of his back. He smelled unfamiliar in this sudden proximity, a strange sweet smell like apricots. His lips moved against her neck. The blood was rushing in her ears. He slid his hands beneath her shirt, tentatively touched her breasts. The image came to her, unbidden, of Sharona and her plump white hands, so different from her own. She let him pull her shirt off over her head, lifting her arms like a child, and waited while he unbuttoned his. He pushed her backward onto the bed, pressing his lips and tongue to hers, urgent, awkward, her nipples hard against his chest, his weight pressing her down. It was only after he had unzipped her jeans and was pushing his fingers inside that she grasped his arm and said, Gavi, no.

He rolled off her onto his back, covering his eyes with his arm.

I'm sorry, she said.

She sat up and swung her feet to the floor, her upper body bare and cold, her jeans flapped open at the waist. She wanted to say something, but there were no words. She felt his need radiating toward her like a star. She reached back and rested her hand on his thigh. He turned his head and gave her a glancing look like a stone skipping across water and shifted his leg away.

I'm so sorry, she said again.

He said, It's okay.

They pulled their shirts back on in silence, the afternoon light watery and gray behind the blinds. He went into the bathroom and she heard the pull-chain toilet flush, water running in the sink. Their grandmother would be waiting. How much time had passed?

When he came out, she said, We'd better go.

Out on the street, it had begun to rain, a spring rain that splattered in plump drops onto the sidewalk, leaving round wet stains. The air was sweet with the smell of ozone.

Susan told herself, Eleanor Roosevelt married her cousin. Even first cousins got married all the time. No one was talking about marriage anyhow.

The fact was nothing happened. Still, she was left with a wretched, guilty aftertaste and a shattered feeling inside, like the aftermath of an explosion.

She didn't tell anyone about it, and she and Gavi didn't speak of it again. But the secret fact of it hovered between them like an aura. From time to time, she thought of the two of them as children, mugging for the camera. Once she'd told him that she was a witch and that if they crossed their eyes and held sticks between their teeth the picture wouldn't come out. But, of course, it did.

It was just a few months later that Susan's mother called her with the news. Susan took the call in the newsroom from her desk, pressing a finger against one ear.

He's been sleeping outside in the garden, her mother said. He won't eat anything Sharona cooks. He hasn't gone in to work for weeks.

Susan pressed her arm against the space beneath her ribs. She should have known.

It's taken everybody by surprise, her mother said. What do you think? Did anything ever seem strange to you?

Susan said, Not really, no.

Your uncle says Gavi won't acknowledge that anything is wrong, her mother said, and that isn't a good sign. Apparently, he's gone back to this "group" of his, but won't talk about it at all. Sharona has moved out. Who can blame her? It's a terrible thing.

Susan logged on to the computer and found an article that described a group whose followers believed in the mystical meaning of numbers and colors, in the connection between all things. They believed in astrology, astral travel, tarot, reincarnation. They didn't live in communes, but held secret meetings in which they meditated to cleanse their auras. They thought the world was evil and bound to destroy itself. They believed there was no such thing as coincidence or chance.

They believed that everything had meaning. Every shape, number, word. The phenomenal world was no more or less than a vast labyrinth of messages waiting to be decoded, understood. The idea was not unfamiliar to Susan; didn't the Kabbalist mystics think in this same way? A teacup might denote nurturing or creation, containment—or emptiness, if you considered the "zero" of its rim. And what about the handle, so like a human ear?

There was a certain paranoia, surely, to viewing the world as a network of signification encoded in cryptic signs.

Susan found the photograph of Gavi with strange eyes taken on the night of their coincidental encounter at the airport six years before and pinned it to the bulletin board above her desk. Susan's parents reported that Sharona had filed for divorce. Gavi had moved back into his parents' flat. All he does is sit on the couch all day and watch TV, Susan's father said.

Susan didn't call Gavi, even though she wanted to. She was afraid there wasn't anything to say. She looked up at the photograph instead. She didn't think he was crazy, but it was impossible to tell. People had breakdowns, didn't they? She wondered when she'd see him again. Her grandmother was moving to a nursing home on the *merkaz*; the flat would soon be sold. Before long, her grandmother, too, would probably be dead. What reason would she have to go to Israel then?

In her memory, Susan is standing at the Panorama Street railing, looking down the Carmel onto the golden dome of the Baha'i Temple, the elaborate sloping gardens lined with cypresses, the red roofs of the German Colony, the cluster of tall buildings on the Hadar. The long arc of Haifa bay curves north past the oil refineries and white storage drums, up to the faint gleam of the chalk cliffs at Rosh Hanikra, the border of southern Lebanon. The sea is blue and flat as glass. She misses it, and without her realizing it the longing has shattered inside her, leaving small invisible cuts like thorns. It is spring. Jays chatter in the pines above her head. Anemones push through the swaying grass. Far off, there is the murmur of a radio, the clink of cutlery, a barking dog.

reunification

The Berlin Wall came down the year that they broke up. Her ex-boyfriend sent her photographs, a whole roll of film, close-ups of the graffiti, swirls and curves and curlicues, like strange ideograms.

He sent pictures of his new apartment, too, a soaring empty space with bare floors and windows set at odd angles on white walls. He was paring down to essentials. From the bedroom, he wrote, he could see Kaiser Wilhelm's Gedächtniskirche, the bombed-out church against a fractured sky.

Susan tried to imagine herself in that space, hollow and symbolic, against the walls left standing, the walls torn down. She'd moved into a boxy one bedroom on the thirtieth floor of a postwar high-rise on the Upper West Side, and from where she sat, all you could see was air.

When she turned the letter over, she saw that he'd signed it *Auf wiedersehen*.

German was her father's mother tongue, but after the war, in Palestine, he changed his name from Fritz to Ezra and forgot most of his German, though he kept his accent. Susan was so used to it that she hardly noticed, but sometimes, when friends of hers who didn't know him spoke to him on the phone, they'd say, Where's he from?

Susan's grandparents lived in Israel, but spoke German to each other and English to Susan and her brothers, switching to German when they didn't want them to understand. They all avoided complex topics as a result, sticking to a simple vocabulary, enunciating with care and much waving of hands.

Although Susan's mother urged her to take French (the language of culture, she said), Susan signed up for German her freshman year in college. The instructor was a buxom woman, with thick forearms and a mole on her left eyelid. You have a natural accent! she told Susan, complimenting her on her name: *Stern*, she told the class, pronouncing the first consonant with a *sh* sound, means "star."

After a week or two, Susan decided her mother was right. She dropped the class and took French instead.

Susan's ex-boyfriend called, long distance, from Berlin. He was upset. He said that the woman he'd been dating was pregnant. Things hadn't been serious between them at all, he told Susan, but now the woman wanted him to marry her.

This is not the way it was supposed to be, he said. This changes everything.

Susan carried the phone over to the window and looked down at the flowing Hudson as the late afternoon sky turned the color of a bruise. She tried to picture him sitting at his glass table, surrounded by those high white walls. She thought: not such an empty apartment. Not just the essentials, after all.

Look, she said, this is your kid we're talking about. This could be the best thing that ever happened to you.

Her voice sounded calm and wise in her ears, as if it belonged to someone else. She'd always thought that if she got pregnant unexpectedly she'd have an abortion, but as she spoke she realized that she probably wouldn't, after all.

I miss you, Susan, her ex-boyfriend said. You always know the right thing to say.

Back in journalism school, when Susan and her ex-boyfriend were first in love, the world had seemed to be a fixed and fathomable place, as predictable as a map. Back then, the Soviet Union was the Evil Empire and Star Wars a defense initiative. They laughed at Wolfgang, a Poly Sci Ph.D. candidate from Düsseldorf who was writing a dissertation on the reunification of Germany. They sat around on sagging couches with their feet up on plank-and-milk-crate coffee tables and shook their heads, laughing, over bottles of imported beer.

Wolfie, Wolfie, Wolfie, they said. It will never happen!

Of course, Susan knew that her great-grandfather, her mother's *zeyde* from Lwów, had once said the same thing about refrigeration, about air travel, about the Second World War.

Susan's grandmother had a cousin who had lost a child in the war. The boy had been the oldest of her three children, and her husband had arranged to get him out of Germany ahead of the rest of the family, alone. The child was barely six. They stood and waved good-bye to him from the platform at the Friedrich-straße Bahnhof in Berlin. They never saw nor heard from him again.

The International Red Cross had tried to reunite the children lost in the war with their relatives, posting photographs of the foundlings in railway stations across Europe and reading their names over daily radio broadcasts. Now, more than fifty years after the war's end, there were still thousands of unclaimed children—not children any longer, of course, but men and women well past middle age. The Red Cross was no longer receiving much of a response.

Susan's grandmother kept photographs of her sons as children tucked beneath the glass top of her vanity. Susan studied the pictures while her grandmother puffed powder on her cheeks, papery as crepe, and filled in her eyebrows with pencil. The photographs were posed studio portraits, black-and-white faded to tones of gray. Susan's father and his brother had chin-length hair tied with bows, like girls. They bore no resemblance to the men Susan knew, as if they'd come from another century, another world. She wondered if her grandmother's cousin kept photographs of her vanished child. She pictured him with protruding ears and a dimple in his chin, like a pinhole or a star. She wanted to ask her grandmother if she thought the boy could possibly still be alive, but she didn't have the nerve.

Susan's grandmother never talked about the war. What she talked about, instead, was her own girlhood. She told stories about how she fought with her sister (the prettier, cleverer, unlucky one), rode in the sidecar of her boyfriend's motorcycle, brought her dolls along on her honeymoon. Her stories had morals, like fairy tales.

She told the same stories, over and over, so that after a while it no longer seemed that they were true.

Susan's ex-boyfriend didn't marry his pregnant girlfriend, but he didn't leave her, either. In the end, she had a baby girl. He sent Susan a photograph. In it he was standing next to a baby carriage. All you could see inside the carriage was a bundle of pale pink. Her ex-boyfriend was wearing a herringbone wool overcoat and a college scarf wound around his neck. He stood slightly hunched over the carriage with an anxious, impatient expression on his face, as if the baby might be crying and he wasn't certain what to do. In the background was a broad, gray street lined with leafless trees.

Linden trees, perhaps.

Susan's father went to a conference in Germany when she was in grade school, not long after the Munich Olympics. It was his first trip back since he was a boy.

When he got home, he said, A tall man in a uniform came to meet me at the airport. He stepped forward and said, Herr Stern.

Herr Stern.

It was only the driver, her father said. But it gave me a little chill.

Susan's ex-boyfriend was twenty-eight when they met, six years older than she: an older man. He'd traveled, held a real job, even lived with another woman for a time. He was ready, he said, to settle down. From the beginning, she felt the pull of gravity.

The first time she went to his parents' house, they sat on his childhood bed and he showed her his high school track trophies, his Princeton yearbook, souvenirs from trips to Nouakchott and

Johannesburg, and she felt as if he were laying it all out for her, a life he could superimpose on hers, like a transparency over a photograph.

They slept together in the guest room on a sleigh bed with scars on the footboard left by a cowboy ancestor's spurs. Susan lay next to him in a darkness that smelled of old books and musty chenille and imagined the way their children would be. She wanted it all: the trophies, the ancestors, the sensation she got of being safe in his orbit, her feet held firmly to the ground.

Susan's grandparents were fond of her ex-boyfriend. Her grandmother said he was *sehr schön*. Her grandfather called him a *mensch*.

When her grandparents came for a visit to New York, they sat around her parents' dinner table while her grandfather told stories Susan had never heard before about the First World War and fighting the Italians at Monte Grappa in the Dolomites. Her grandfather grew animated, sketching diagrams and maps on scraps of paper and waving his hands. When Susan got up to clear the dishes, she heard her ex-boyfriend laugh and her grandfather say, Ah, you understand me exactly!

When she asked her grandfather why he'd never told her the stories before, he said, Because you never asked.

Susan went to buy a gift for her ex-boyfriend's baby. As she stood in the plush Amsterdam Avenue shop, fingering the Steiff bunnies and satin-edged blankets and tiny crocheted booties, the door jingled and her ex-boyfriend's college roommate walked in. She hid the booties behind her back, as if she'd been caught in the act of doing something shameful.

The college roommate kissed her on the cheek. I was over in Berlin last month, he said, and I'm telling you, this woman is a piece of work. She just wanted to catch herself an American.

Susan noticed that his hair had thinned, leaving a round patch on the top of his scalp, like a yarmulke. He worked for the U.S. attorney's office, prosecuting white-collar crime. In the old days, the three of them had hung out together in dive bars on the Lower East Side.

He sure made a mistake not marrying you, the college roommate said, touching Susan's arm, even though he knew perfectly well that she was the one who'd done the breaking up.

Susan's ex-boyfriend was, in fact, half-Jewish. His father's relatives came from Dresden by way of Brooklyn; the cowboys and Ivy Leaguers were all on his mother's side. Her ex-boyfriend's family celebrated Christmas and Easter, though not in a religious way. His brother, however, was a Scientologist. He believed in a tone scale of emotion and the traumatic residue of past lives. Susan's mother considered this a bad sign, just as, although she didn't say anything directly, she felt that Susan's ex-boyfriend didn't count as a real Jew.

That's what happens, she said when Susan told her about the brother, when you don't have real roots.

The summer between their two years of journalism school, Susan and her ex-boyfriend went to Poland. Wolfgang, who was in Warsaw doing research, took them around. It was their first time behind the Iron Curtain.

Wolfie drove his beat-up Volkswagen Golf at high rates of speed along rutted country roads, swerving around bicycles and horse-drawn carts piled high with hay. An orange sun hovered low in the sky. A haze of burning coal clouded the air.

On the way from Warsaw to Krakow, they stopped at Auschwitz. It was late afternoon and the klieg lights above the double—barbed wire fence had come on, casting shadows on the ground. Above the gate, the sign remained: *Arbeit Macht Frei*. Rows of cypresses lined the paths like sentries. There was hardly anyone there. Susan's ex-boyfriend shot a roll of black-and-white film. Wolfgang stuffed his hands into his pockets and looked at his feet. Nobody said much.

Susan wandered around thinking about her grandmother's cousin and her lost child, wondering what had become of him. She thought about her grandmother's sister—the prettier, cleverer, unluckier one—after whom she had been named. The fact that she'd probably died here in this place felt as unreal as any other family story.

They climbed back into Wolfie's Volkswagen and continued on to Krakow. After checking into the hotel, Susan and her ex-boyfriend made love on the narrow Soviet-style bed.

Ibusz, he crooned as he kissed her breasts. It was the name of the Polish state travel agency, but they'd decided it sounded like a term of endearment. He put on a fake accent and addressed her nipple. You are my leetle Polish radish, he said. Then they went out for dinner.

Her ex-boyfriend proposed to her at the end of that year, a few days after they finished their exams. They were sitting in Central Park watching the sun drop behind the apartment buildings on the Upper West Side. He turned to face her and placed his hand on her knee.

I know this changes everything, he said. But I wanted you to know how I feel.

Susan said she needed to think it over, and for the next two and a half years, she thought it over, until it came to seem that they had, in fact, gotten married and were already contemplating divorce. She had a dream in which she was standing in full white bridal dress alone on a stage in the center of an enormous stadium, surrounded by a crowd of strangers. The ring on her finger was as big as a bracelet and made of steel. She stood searching in vain for her ex-boyfriend, thinking, This isn't the way it was supposed to be.

Even now, looking back, Susan was never quite sure how they lost each other, how the familiar became strange, the way even a common word starts to sound foreign if you repeat it too many times out loud. Gravity failed them, after all. Even so, in the last months, before she finally moved out, and before he left for Berlin, she kept imagining that if he'd just ask her to marry him again, everything would be okay, but he never did.

Not long after her ex-boyfriend's baby was born, Susan met a Swedish artist at a party and let him take her home with him. His loft was filled with the heads of angels, molded in rough clay. They gazed down with wide, vacant eyes, tilted gently toward one another as if dreaming or entranced. In candlelight diffuse with clay dust, the sculptor covered her body with fluttering kisses. He had a long body, fair skin, eyebrows so pale they were almost invisible. His blond hair swung forward over Susan's face as he moved. With a tremor of what she took to be excitement in his voice, he told her it was the first time he'd ever slept with a Jewish girl.

Susan's ex-boyfriend called from his parents' house in Washington, D.C. He was there for a week with the baby, visiting.

I wish you could meet her, he said. She's a big part of my life, now.

Susan flew down the following Saturday morning. She'd cut her hair, and as the cab pushed through the traffic on Massachusetts Avenue, she wondered if she looked different. They hadn't seen each other in almost three years.

Her ex-boyfriend stepped out onto the front stoop as the cab pulled up. He was holding his daughter on his hip. Her ex-boyfriend had brown hair and eyes, like Susan, but the baby had white-blond ringlets and eyes as blue as the sky. She looked like a Botticelli angel—as Aryan as you could get. Susan felt a sharp jolt of surprise.

Say hi to Papa's friend, her ex-boyfriend cooed. The child burrowed her face against her father's neck. He stroked her curls and muttered some words in German that Susan couldn't understand. It hadn't occurred to her that the child would speak German, although it made perfect sense.

The baby was fussy and cried when Susan held her, arching her back. Susan handed her back to her ex-boyfriend, feeling as though she'd failed some kind of test, and then they stood in the kitchen making conversation with his parents, just like in the old days. Susan wondered if his parents thought they might be getting back together again, and then she wondered if that was why she'd come.

Finally, her ex-boyfriend put the child to bed, and they left her with her grandparents and went out to get Thai food.

So what do you think? her ex-boyfriend said.

Susan looked around at the gold embroidered elephants marching along the restaurant's walls. She's a cute kid, she said.

I think she's doing amazingly well, considering, her ex-boyfriend said. He picked at the label of his beer bottle, making a pile of soggy gold shreds beside his plate. He rolled the shreds between his fingers, looking down, concentrating, and Susan watched his hands. They were honest hands, with veins that ran blue over wrists as slender as a woman's, a smudge of ink on the side of the palm, a few stoic hairs as placeholders on the finger where a ring should be. They were the hands, she reminded herself, of the father of someone else's nineteen-month-old girl.

What, "considering"? she said.

Well, considering the whole situation, the whole damn mess, the whole way it's not supposed to be.

Oh right, Susan said. Not the white picket fence and the two-point-five kids and the perfect little wife.

He looked up at her, pressed his lips together in a line. You just don't get it, do you, he said.

After the breakup, Susan had dated one man after another, all eligible and Jewish but phobic of commitment and neurotic in bed. Friends fixed her up with a forensic psychiatrist, a software entrepreneur with a cocaine habit, a venture capitalist, a rabbinical candidate. Twice, she was fixed up with the same man, an overweight district attorney with a mouth like a fish.

Her parents never nagged her about her unmarried state, but Susan knew they were concerned. It was grandchildren they wanted, continuation of the line. Only once, when she mentioned a friend from high school who'd recently had a baby, her mother said, Honey, you are going to be the last of the Mohicans.

When Susan and her ex-boyfriend returned to his parents' house, the place was dark and his parents had gone to bed. They stood by the kitchen sink, sipping glasses of water, like two people at the intermission of a play.

Her ex-boyfriend offered her the guest room or the attic. She said, The attic's fine.

She followed him up two flights of stairs to a daybed wedged under the eaves, surrounded by dusty stacks of magazines and baskets of old toys. It was a hot night, and the attic was at least ten degrees hotter than the rest of the house. He pushed open a dormer window, which gave out a creak and a breath of dust.

He brushed his hands on his jeans. Are you sure you'll be okay?

She said, It's fine.

They stood there for a moment and then Susan stepped forward, even though she'd vowed she wouldn't, and he put his arms around her, pressing her face against his shirt. Then he pulled back and let his hands drop to his sides.

Sleep tight, he said.

After he left, Susan stretched out on the daybed, fully dressed, and listened to the sound of running water and the creaking of doors downstairs. She tried not to think about the two of them asleep below, the child among the old trophies and yearbooks, her ex-boyfriend in the sleigh bed that had once been theirs, his feet on the marks of a dead cowboy's spurs.

An old black-and-white photograph hung in the hallway in Susan's grandparents' Haifa flat, a picture of a group of people in bathing suits posing on a beach. In the center, a man stood with his hands on the shoulders of two women, the man in the kind of black one-piece swimming costume, like an acrobat's leotard, that was the fashion around the turn of the last century, the women in short-sleeved cotton frocks tied with string sashes at the waist, printed kerchiefs on their heads. The women were on tiptoe, their heels raised off the ground, as if they were slowly levitating. Between the women, three children sat in a descending line, their hands on each other's shoulders, the youngest one, a girl, holding a doll. Everyone was smiling except the little girl—Susan's grandmother—and her doll. If you looked closely, you could see that the doll's mouth was open, her arms up by her head, her legs bent and kicking in the air, as if she were trying to wrench herself free from Susan's grandmother's grasp and cartwheel down the sand.

In a dream, Susan is last in line in this upside-down pyramid, seated cross-legged at her grandmother's feet, her grandmother's hands on her shoulders, and she is holding the doll. There she sits on that sunny summer afternoon, on that vanished European beach, thinking how it is so peaceful and familiar, until she looks down and realizes that what she is holding isn't a doll, but a baby, its arms and legs as stiff as plastic, its eyes squeezed shut, its mouth frozen open in a soundless cry.

On Sunday afternoon, her ex-boyfriend drove her to the airport in his father's car. He pulled the sunroof back and drove in silence past the stately rows of government buildings, the dome of the Capitol shining on the hill, the long scar of the Vietnam War Memorial cut into the Constitution Gardens grass.

I've decided to move back to the States, he finally said.

Susan turned to look at him. With the kid?

He shook his head, his eyes fixed on the road, his lips pressed together in a line, as they'd been the night before. Susan wanted to reach across the gearshift to take his hand, but there was something about the pain in his eyes, the set of his mouth, that made her stop.

It was only later, as her plane lifted and banked over the shimmering Potomac, that Susan let herself think back to that moment in Central Park, that question hanging unanswered between them in the cooling air.

When Susan finally went to Berlin, a couple of years later, her ex-boyfriend had long since moved away. She walked along the Kurfürstendamm her first night there, through the neon lights and jostling crowds. She passed a woman walking with a little girl with fair curly hair and a familiar tilt to her eyes, and she turned back for another look even though this child was much younger than her ex-boyfriend's daughter would have been by now. She sat for a while at the edge of the fountain and looked up at Kaiser Wilhelm's ruined church, its hollow tower floodlit from below, like a stage set, and then went back to her hotel.

The wall itself was long gone, of course, and the Potsdamer Platz had turned from a mine-filled no-man's-land into the largest construction site in the world. Of the city her grandparents had known, there was hardly a trace. Cranes and scaffolding stretched across the sky. She walked all the way around the square, feeling the way she always did when she traveled alone: invisible and weightless and free.

Before she left, she bought a postcard at a kiosk. She sat in a café and addressed it to her ex-boyfriend. She thought about writing, *Thinking of you*. She thought about writing, *Auf wiedersehen*. In the end, she put it in her purse and didn't write anything at all.

I look everywhere for grandmothers and find none.

ELIZABETH BARRETT BROWNING

LILA'S STORY

Israel 1997

In my memory, my grandmother is framed by flowers. Head-high
stalks of gladioli, a backdrop of hibiscus, anemones at her feet.
My grandmother is smiling, cheek to bloom. Here are the flowers
still: tricolor lantana bordering the sidewalk, vermilion bougain-
villea overhanging the second-story stairs. Here are photographs,
a pile of black-and-white snapshots taken in the 1940s, not long
after my grandparents arrived in Palestine. I flip through them
like tarot cards, lay them face up on my hotel room bed. Here is my
grandmother in a full skirt and blouse and walking shoes, kneeling
in the Carmel woods called Little Switzerland. Here she is, arms
linked with her two sons, posing on the beach. She is beautiful, or
almost, cat-eyed and slim, with an aquiline nose and prematurely
white hair. Here she is leaning against a railing by the sea. Her hair
is blowing across her face and she is squinting just a bit. The sea behind her is flecked with white. The camera has caught that fleeting
moment that precedes the self-consciousness of a smile, and that,

with that slight squint and windblown hair, makes her look contemplative and a little reckless, both vulnerable and brave. I sweep the photographs back into a pile, leaving this one on the top.

Palestine 1939

Lila knows it isn't true the world is round. The ship from Trieste pitched forward and fell right off the edge. The gulls wheeled up off the deck and screamed into the wind. Here in Haifa, it is primitive, dusty, dirty, hot. It is the Orient, the Levant, the Near East but not nearly near enough. The road they live on is unpaved. Only cold water from the tap. Lila boils the drinking water, scrubs the fruit and vegetables with soap, makes sure to toast the bread. She pores over the notebook her cook gave her when they left, recipes handwritten in a slanting German scrawl. She cooks in the heat of the afternoon while Josef takes his nap—the kind of food they're used to, too heavy for this climate—Wiener schnitzel, potato salad, a chocolate roulade. It is just so *uncivilized*, she writes to her sister in a letter she will never read. Everyone wears khaki shirts and shorts—even the girls! You see women squatting by the roadside, breaking paving stones, while Herr Doktor Professor drives a bus. Even Josef has had to take work selling curtains door to door. There are fedayeen and jackals in the hills. At night, the jackals come down into the wadi behind our house; you can hear them howling at the moon.

Lila's Story

Everything was so difficult for me then. The boys ran wild; I wasn't used to doing everything myself. Back home, you understand, I had my cook and nanny, my parents and my sister close to me. So I thought I would be happier living on a kibbutz. I would do any work they wanted me to do—picking oranges at dawn, or weeding in the fields—in exchange for the communal kitchen and dining hall, the children's quarters, the company of friends. We went to visit Deganya and I was so enthusiastic, I couldn't stop talking about it for days. But your grandfather said no. We are not socialists or Bolsheviks, he said. It is not what we are used to. It is not our way. And, of course, he was right.

Merkaz

Back in Haifa for the first time since her death, I retrace my grandmother's steps. I've been coming here since I was a child, and it's a child's universe I know: the shady playground in the Gan Ha'em; Panorama Street with its picture-postcard view; the shortcut, slippery with dead pine needles, around the back of my grandparents' old flat. I walk up Hanassi toward the town center, the *merkaz*, the way my grandmother did each day: past the Delek station on the corner, past the soldiers smoking outside the barracks gate, past the Dan Carmel and Panorama hotels, past Goldman's art gallery, an indoor mall, the entrance to the Carmelit. I pass an ice-cream shop, a pizza parlor, branches of the banks Leumi and Hapoalim. Here at the corner there used to be a handbag shop, dim and pungent with the smell of leather hides. Next door, now gone as well, there was a toy store stacked with dolls in cardboard boxes crinkly with cellophane. Across the street, Mr. Schaeffer's market is still there, although someone else in a white apron is standing by the door. Here, around the corner, is Steimatsky's, the English-language bookstore, and here's the newsstand where my grandmother bought me treats—I remember the Bazooka bubble gum with Hebrew comic strips, glass bottles of Fanta with paper straws that unraveled when they got wet, the bars of Elite chocolate my grandmother liked best. Further on, up the hill, are more cafés, the concert hall, the tennis club, a shady park. There, I sat on a bench in the late afternoon while my grandmother told stories. An Egged bus pulls away from the light with a black cloud of exhaust. The air smells of diesel fumes, of pine and eucalyptus, of garbage ripening in the sun. Childhood smells. So are these my grandmother's footsteps or my own?

Palestine 1941

Lila walks with her three dogs: a spaniel, a terrier, and a little white one of indeterminate breed. Her bunions hurt but she ignores the pain. No, she doesn't ignore it—the pain is what reminds her she's alive. The dogs sniff at the wooden crates of produce at the grocer's tin-roofed stand. She buys a loaf of bread, a wedge of cheese, some tomatoes, cucumbers, and grapes. There's no real coffee these days, not even Nescafé. Some days she has to force herself to eat. She counts out the money carefully in German; the tinny coins all look the same. She carries the groceries in a string bag, which cuts into her palms. Across the *merkaz*, she climbs the steps to the post office, checks the box. There's not often mail from home. From time to time a thin blue aerogram arrives from London, from one of Josef's sisters there. Lila tells herself that it rains too much in England, that even Britain is no longer any place for Jews. Of course, the British are here, too, red-kneed and stiff in their high socks and shorts. They smile at her dogs. They are too polite to smile at her; even the younger ones avert their eyes.

Lila's Story

We were very lucky. From a cousin, we got entrance papers for Palestine. He was a doctor and by this time the Nazis no longer permitted him to leave. Josef's sisters went to England; his parents were, *Gott sei Danke*, by then already dead. My parents and sister stayed behind. They believed, *nebekh*, that everything would be all right. My sister was much more beautiful and clever than I, only she had no luck. We learned, after the war, that my parents were sent to Theresienstadt in 1942. My father died there, but my mother was sent on a transport from Theresienstadt to Auschwitz on October 23, 1944—imagine, only days before the gas chambers were shut down, weeks before the liberation of the camp. What became of my sister, I do not know.

View

Back at the hotel, I cross the shiny lobby floor, past the tour groups waiting amid piles of luggage, past the buzz around the front desk. It is strange staying at the Dan Carmel alone, but my aunt and uncle's place is small, and of course my grandparents' flat is gone. I take the elevator to the sixth floor. My grandmother never rode in elevators; even in her eighties, she always took the stairs. The doors open to a wall-sized blown up photograph of the Old City in Jerusalem, peeling where it's come unglued along the center splice. The view from my room, onto Haifa bay, is another classic tourist shot. I push aside the drapes and step out on the balcony into the failing light. I can see out over Panorama Street to the golden dome of the Baha'i Temple, its gardens spilling down the mountainside; a glimpse of the taller buildings on the Hadar; and to the north, the oil refineries' storage drums, the curved arm of the coast. As the sky fades from pink to gray, lights begin to twinkle from the battlements of the U.S. Sixth Fleet gunships at anchor in the bay.

I go back inside and pick up the pile of old photographs my aunt has given me, shuffle through them one more time. Here is the one of my grandmother leaning against that railing by the sea. She is smiling, her head tipped back, her lips slightly parted, as if she were about to speak. There is a flower—a narcissus, maybe—in her hand. If she had looked up then, she would have seen the ridgeline of the Carmel, green with cypresses and olive trees and pines. She would have been looking at the spot where this hotel now stands. Now she gazes up through time at me and I gaze down at her. What am I looking for? Something tiny in the background—a half-glimpsed face, an out-of-focus sign. A footprint, a fingerprint, a trace of scent, a follicle of hair.

No. I am looking for myself.

Palestine 1941

So you could say that they survived, but they were not *survivors*, not exactly, not in the new sense of the word. They were never in the camps. They never had to hide out in a gentile's barn or forage in the forest with the partisans. They were not displaced persons— not officially, anyway—even though they were among the refugees, the dispossessed. They were immigrants, among the lucky ones. Lila had packed their belongings in trunks and crates—a wooden angel that had hung over her boys' crib for luck, an oil painting of the Weinerwald, her dolls, her gilt-edged dinner service for sixteen, a Gallé table lamp, their goose-down quilts, the bedroom set her parents gave them when they were married, several reels of sixteen-millimeter film containing footage of ski trips to Kitzbühel and Zürs, her jewelry, a gold watch, her silverware engraved with her initials, a box of photographs, thirty-two Moser crystal goblets—and they set sail for Haifa, as if they were going on a holiday. They were Europeans, not exactly Zionists, but there was no escaping being Jews. Now they were yekkes, German-speaking Jews, with their poor Hebrew and assimilated Prussian ways. They were always punctual, drank *Kaffe mit Schlag* in the *merkaz* cafés, kept their jackets on even in the stifling summer heat. The old Russian socialists, who had been in Palestine for generations, made fun of the yekkes, of their stiffness and bewilderment and fear. Everyone was talking about the new Jews, the pioneers, which all their children would doubtless be. The posters showed blond, blue-eyed, snub-nosed kibbutzniks grinning in the sun. The yekkes had never seen Jews like these before. These boys and girls had sun-bronzed skin and calloused hands. They worked the land. They would fight back. They would show the world.

Lila's Story

Things were different by us, back home. We were Jewish but we were not religious, do you understand? We had many wonderful friends. In the winter, we went skiing—in those days, you climbed up and passed the night in a hut, then skied down the next day—and ice skating in the park. We went mushroom picking in the forest in the spring. When I first knew your grandfather, he took me on his motorbike. He told me that once he'd lost a girlfriend off the back—he found her later, of course, back at her parents' house, but as you can imagine she refused to speak to him. Later, he got a sidecar, and we used to say that when we had a baby we would put it in the sidecar in a basket, tied on with a bow! Of course, we never did. By then we had a car.

The Married Man

The last time I saw my grandmother, just over a year ago, she was in a nursing home and my grandfather had been dead for nearly six years. I sat on the only chair and she sat on the single bed. She smoothed her knotty hands over her skirt, a girlish gesture. Her shoulders curved forward and the skin hung in wrinkled folds along her neck. But her faded gray-green eyes were clear. Do you ever wish you'd married him? she asked. We were talking about my ex-boyfriend. No, I said, although the truth was I wasn't sure. How could you be? He was married to someone else now and had a child. You don't have to get married, my grandmother said. I just wouldn't want you to end up old and all alone. Israelis marry young; at thirty-three, I know she thought that I was over the hill. Although it's possible, of course, that she was just thinking about herself. There was a sweater folded by her pillow, a gray V-neck that had been my grandfather's and that, she told me, still retained a faint trace of his smell. I speak with him every night, she said. By all accounts, my grandparents loved each other well. As long as I knew them, they called each other by the same pet name—*mükki, mükki*—as if they were reciprocals of one another, two parts of the same whole.

I didn't tell my grandmother about the man I was seeing at the time. The man was married, though I didn't think of what we were having as an affair. I never wanted him to leave his wife and kids for me. I wasn't really in love with him, although later, after it was over, I felt betrayed. He once told me that he knew we'd be close forever, and so I had pictured the two of us, mellow and gray, side by side in rocking chairs on a weather-beaten porch, looking out at rolling hills. In reality, what we had together was sex. You are the ultimate mind fuck, he once said. I was needy enough, at the time, to take this comment as a compliment.

Palestine 1941

Lila sits at her dressing table, brushing her hair. She puts on lipstick, rolling the crimson tube so it tapers to a point. She rubs pencil across her brows, pats powder on her cheeks and nose. In the mirror, she considers her face. At thirty-seven, her hair is almost completely white, although she dyes it black leaving just one white streak in front. Her face is approaching that borderland between youth and age, her cheekbones and jawline more angular than they used to be, faint lines tracing her smile and her frown. Pressed beneath the glass of her dressing table, next to photographs of her parents and her sons, she keeps an edelweiss Josef gave her years ago for luck—an albino fallen star. She thinks back to those early days, before they were married, when she'd tell her parents she was going to see her best friend, Hanni, but would meet up with him instead. Their tongues touched with the urgency of disobedience and little lies. He wore a brown wool overcoat. He curved around her like a spiral shell. They walked slowly, arms wrapped around each other's waists, under leafy chestnuts and spreading firs, under a sky bleached white with scudding clouds. Later, she found that he would often walk ahead. He walked steadily, stubbornly, like the Great War officer he had been, never breaking pace to rest or run ahead, while she (taking off a sweater, putting it back on again) skipped along behind. But it was true that where the path got rough or steep, he would wait to take her hand. Now she touches the edelweiss with one finger through the glass. Edelweiss doesn't grow here in the Holy Land. Here she has to search for other talismans—a night-blooming cereus, a hidden violet in the spring.

Lila's Story

When I married, I was just a girl. I was twenty-four but I didn't know anything. Do you understand? Things were not then as they are now. It was the fashion at the time to go to Venice on one's honeymoon. I cried the whole way on the train. Such a silly child I was! I'd brought my dolls with me—my father was furious, saying that I was a married woman now, that I must leave such child's toys at home. But Josef just laughed and said, No, no, let her take what she wants. When we arrived at the hotel, I arranged the dolls by my pillow on the bed. Then I went into the bathroom, and I stayed there for a long time, preparing myself. When I came out at last, I was afraid your grandfather would be angry with me. But then I saw that he had taken my doll—she was beautiful, with dark hair and green glass eyes—and had pinned a diamond brooch onto her dress. Then I was very happy.

Beach

On Shabbat, we go down to the beach, my aunt and uncle and I, my cousins and their wives and kids. Only Gavi doesn't come along. He's moved into a new place downtown by the port. We've spoken briefly on the phone since I've been here, but so far haven't made plans to meet. Every time I think of him, I feel a twinge like wire twisting in my chest.

My aunt and uncle have five grandchildren now, ranging in age from six and a half to two. We walk along the concrete boardwalk at Hof Hacarmel Beach, find a sunny spot, sit down on the sand. It's still early spring and the beach isn't crowded; there's only a small group of old men, brown as cowhide, sunning themselves on folding chairs. The children run back and forth with buckets of water and yell and scream. My uncle says, It's a pity Mother isn't here. Even though the oldest kids already know enough English to communicate with me, the smaller ones are friendliest. The two-year-old charges back and forth between her mother and me, fistfuls of sand draining through her fingers as she runs. *Bevakasha!* she pants, unfurling her hand over my lap. *Todah*, I say. We do this again and again.

The married man had children, too; at the time we were involved, his first was not yet two. Sometimes he'd bring her along when we met, carrying her in a backpack; people who saw us assumed we were a family. He'd touch and kiss me as if the baby weren't there. I shouldn't have let him, but I did. I knew the baby understood. She fixed me with a steady open stare, as if to say, don't take what isn't yours. So later, when the man cried on my shoulder and said he didn't know if he could bear to leave his kids, I told him he should stay with them.

Palestine 1941

Although Josef has said he doesn't want another child, Lila gets pregnant not long after they come to Palestine. She isn't careless on purpose, but it isn't exactly an accident either. She waits for her period as her breasts grow full and tender as a bruise. Over dinner, Josef talks about starting a factory like the one he had before

the war, a knitwear business, manufacturing baby clothes. He will
sell his stamp collection, Josef says, and with the money he got out
before the war he should have enough to lease some space, buy
machines. Once the war is over, he says. Once the situation with the
British is resolved. It is a matter of time. The boys eat silently and
fast; Josef lets them go. He cuts himself another wedge of cheese,
tears off a piece of bread. Lila wraps her arms around her waist,
takes little sips of wine. She imagines the outfits they'll design:
one-piece suits in yellow and white, tiny booties with pompoms on
the strings. Yellow jacquard sweaters with matching leggings and a
cap. Overalls in red or blue velour with pocket appliqués of dogs.
They will help build this country, Josef says. They will join the ranks
of the *halutzniks*, the pioneers. Lila wonders if this time it will be a
girl. She has hung her wooden angel to the side of the front door. It
looks away from her now, out over her head, its cherub's face tipped
up, a blank expression in its eyes.

Lila's Story

I got pregnant after we came to Palestine, yes. But your grandfather
did not want another child. It was different, he said, when we had
a baby nurse and a nanny and all the family around. Now it would
not be so easy to start again. Not so easy at all. And imagine, I was
nearly forty at the time! I was crazy to think to have another child
then. Crazy! Already we had two beautiful boys, almost fully grown.
So I ended it. It was not difficult to arrange; the country was very
modern for the time. There were plenty of good Jewish doctors
without enough work who were willing to do such a thing. No, it
would have been impossible to keep the child. Your grandfather
was always right.

Photograph

One of the few things I have kept from my time with the married man is a series of photographs of me in a swimming pool in Mexico. I am smiling up from the too-blue water, arms folded over the pool's blue tiled edge, my head tipped back, my hair short and wet. The look on my face could be vanity, or love. I look happy, although I don't remember feeling that way. The man had said, Give me your camera. I want you to see how beautiful you are. I wanted to see myself that way, too, of course. But it was strange, the things you saw or didn't see. Of all the people who later looked at those pictures from my trip to Cozumel, the trip I said I went on all alone, no one ever asked who had taken those photographs of me. It makes me wonder about that photograph of my grandmother with her back turned to the sea. I pick it up and hold it up to the bedside light, and what strikes me now is the faint shadow at her feet. If you look closely, you can just make out the jut of elbows, the curved outline of a head. It makes me wonder, what about that crooked smile, that slight crease between her brows, as she lifts a hand to brush the hair back from her face—as if she were trying to peer backward through the camera's lens to another eye? She wasn't necessarily looking at my grandfather when she smiled that way. Not necessarily, no.

Palestine 1947

From the lookout on Panorama Street, you can see the black plumes of smoke from the refineries that the Stern Gang sabotaged five days before. The smoke billows from the giant oil tanks and spreads out on the wind, an ink-black fog, smudging out the sun. You can smell the burning oil everywhere. Lila stands at the railing with her dogs, looking down at the boulevards of the German Colony, the rooftops of the Hadar, the crooked arm of the northern coast, crosshatched in black. It is March and the hillside is flecked red and blue with flowering sage and flax. Everyone says war is very near. War again. The British have already evacuated their women and children and nonessential men; only police officers and sol-diers remain. Her Fritz is sixteen now, and she holds her fingers crossed that he won't be called to fight. Of course he's dying to join the Palmach. Josef is trying to arrange to send him to textile school in England instead. Then her boy will be gone, but England is bet-ter than a prison cell in Acre, better than the fate of that poor Dov Gruner, who will almost certainly be hanged. The dogs are pulling at their leads, noses to the ground. She turns her head against the acrid wind and starts to walk.

Lev

I want to say that this is where it happens, right here on Panorama Street, under the rustling Carmel pines, in the shadow of what is now this hotel. He walks up and stands beside her, looking out at the conflagration by the shore. He has unruly hair and blazing eyes, a bony concave build. (In a photograph of sixteen early pioneers, he's the one you notice right away, there in the front row, kneeling with one elbow resting on a knobby knee, his deep-set eyes focused right on you.) I want to say that he's a socialist who left Odessa after the First World War, making him almost an old-timer here. I want to call him Lev. So rewind that last scene just a bit. Before the dogs grow impatient and she turns to leave. Instead, she turns and looks at him—he's leaning forward, gazing out at the black plume of smoke, his forearms resting on the rail—and she says (in German, as if to herself), When will it end? And he says, End? (His German isn't bad. Perhaps he studied in Berlin before the war.) But this is just the beginning! She notices his broad forehead, his wild hair, his ropy hands, the intensity of his gaze. Their eyes connect. Maybe nothing happens then, but I want to believe it does. I want to believe that desire rises out of smoke and ruin, out of loneliness and loss. I want to believe that there are infinite cultivars of love.

Lila's Story

Once, when your father was just a baby, your grandfather and I went for a fortnight's skiing holiday to Zürs. It was the first time I'd ever left him, and even though my parents came to stay with him, I was terribly upset. I can't go without my baby! I cried, but your grandfather insisted we leave him home. It will be good to get away, he said, and so we went. At the hotel where we stayed, there was a very nice man from Vienna who took a great liking to me. In the evenings, we played bridge and danced. On my last day, he came to the train station to say good-bye and brought for me an enormous bouquet of flowers. On the train, I held the flowers and I cried. I don't want to go home, I said. Your grandfather said, What? I thought you missed little Fritz so terribly! But the truth is I didn't want to go back at all.

Honey Cake

My aunt and I are sitting at her kitchen table, drinking coffee and picking at the remains of a honey cake. She's trying to talk me into going out with a doctor she's convinced is my perfect match, but I don't want to be fixed up. In a few days, I'll be back home in New York anyway, and I don't like the fact that she is so concerned. He comes from an excellent family, she says, as if that could clinch the deal. She brushes a few crumbs off her chest and lights a cigarette. Look at you, she says, pushing the cake plate over my way. So thin, just like your grandmother. You eat. Of course, we both know what my grandmother was like. She went on a grapefruit diet if she gained a kilo, which must have been rare because as I recall she hardly ate. She never got into a pool without swimming twenty laps. She rose at five, took ice-cold showers long after a gas heater was installed in the flat, rarely sat still for long. She was of another generation, my aunt says. How do you imagine she and your grandfather got along so well? Did you ever hear her once complain? She did everything for *him*. My aunt shakes her head; she is not much of one for mortification of the flesh. She says, So your grandmother got migraine headaches. Sometimes for an entire day she had to stay in bed. For holding everything inside, she says, tapping her chest, there is a cost. But what I want to know is what my grandmother was like *before*—before our memory of her, before the compounded effects of age and time. There is in my pile one photograph of her as a girl of maybe ten or twelve, sitting with her cousin Hansi on a garden bench. For the occasion, they've changed places: she's wearing his leather sandals, his lederhosen, his Tyrolean cap with a feathered brim. He's got on her dirndl (a little tight across the chest), her puff-sleeved blouse, her lace-trimmed socks and low-heeled white shoes. He looks uncomfortable, his hands curled awkwardly in his lap, but she sits triumphant, cocky, round-cheeked, her feet swinging free. She looks as if she might fly up, like Peter Pan, into the trees. Does this make her the kind of woman who would have an affair at forty-three? Really, I know nothing about her at all.

Palestine 1947

Since Haifa, though a city, is really a small town, assume that Lev is only visiting from the kibbutz up north where his ex-wife and three grown sons reside. Assume that the pension where he is staying, run by German Carmelite nuns, is small and out of the way, and that the nuns would have no cause to disbelieve him if he said that Lila was his wife. Assume he's come to Haifa to help organize the resettlement of illegal refugees, who continue to arrive by the thousands, boat by boat, despite the blockade, the deportations, the violence and disease. Remember that everyone is distracted by the approaching war. Remember that Josef is on the road all day and sometimes overnight, that Fritz has sailed for England, that her younger son is still in school. Make the case for opportunity; make the case for need. (Think of her lost parents, sister, baby, her departed son.) Picture the two of them at a café, a few weeks after the Irgun's famous prison raid. Hear her girlish laughter, see them reach across the table to touch hands. A tinny Russian melody is playing on a loudspeaker; hear Lev hum along, a little out of tune. Smell the salty breeze, the ersatz wartime coffee, the faint scent of pine. It is hot. Lev has leaned his motorbike against the wall, where it casts a long shadow on the dusty ground. His camera (a nice new Leica in a leather case) rests on the table by his hand. In a little while, they will get up and stroll a bit along the strand. She will lean against the rail. He will bend to kiss her, then step back. Smile, he will say. I want you to see how beautiful you are.

Lila's Story

When I was sixteen years old, my own grandmother—your great-great-grandmother—died. Like all young girls, I wasn't interested in my grandparents at all. I thought of my grandmother as a terribly old woman always dressed in black, and I ran out of the room as fast as I could whenever she came in. So the biggest effect her death had on me was that my mother, who was in mourning, could no longer accompany my sister and me to our weekly dancing lessons, so my aunt agreed to be our chaperone. Luckily for me, my aunt was always too busy chatting with the other adults to pay much attention to what I was up to. My sister was always well behaved, but I was a terrible flirt, always running off with the boys. This period after my grandmother died was one of the happiest times of my life.

Date

My aunt's doctor friend takes me out for lunch to Isfiya, a Druze village in the hills. The road winds up, the vegetation growing sparse and dry as we leave the sea. The doctor is pale and on the pudgy side, although he speaks English well and is a lively enough companion. We stop at an outdoor restaurant and he orders for us both—falafel and hummus and baba ghanoush, little plates of pickles and olives, a stack of pita bread. Do you know Arabic food? he asks. Do you think I live on the moon? I don't say. Across from where we sit, an Arab villa is going up, with arched windows, a tiled roof, a satellite dish. A Mercedes is parked in front of the piles of dirt. I don't tell him that I've been to Isfiya many times before. Would you ever come to live here? the doctor asks. Would you make aliyah? Israelis often ask me this question. Maybe, I say, although I know now the odds are slim. I doubt the doctor would move even as far away as Tel Aviv. We sit in the lengthening shade of a tree I don't know the name of, lunch almost done, sipping cups of sweet coffee fragrant with cardamom, or *hel*. It doesn't feel like home to me. Of course, I could say that about many places in the States as well.

After the doctor drops me back at the hotel, I go to take a swim. The only other person at the pool is an old woman in a rubber-flowered bathing cap swimming sinking breaststroke laps. I think of the summer I was sixteen when we spent three weeks at this hotel. I hung out by the pool for most of every day. A boy my age did back flips off the diving board while his older brother flirted with me. He was in the army, a paratrooper, he said; he was twenty-two. The edge of my hand brushed against his. He had a solid build, blunt features, greenish eyes like mine. He took me to the beach one afternoon in his orange VW Bug. When my mother found out later, she was irate. I rolled down my window as we drove along the winding mountain road and let the blue wind rush into my face. He rested his right hand on my bare thigh, lifting it only when he had to shift. He parked by the roadside and we walked through the sea grass to the sand. He handed his keys to a woman sitting by the shore. Hold these while I go in the water, he said to her. Don't steal my car, I'm coming back. I ran into him again a few years later, by chance. I was nineteen then and he would have been twenty-five. His skin looked thicker, his eyes smaller, receded into the flesh, as if something vital had been concealed. We snuck out onto the hotel roof and kissed, but it wasn't the same.

Palestine 1948

It is cold, colder in the flat than outside, the tiled floor sending a dull ache up Lila's chilblained shins. They've been forced out of their flat by the British and this new one, on the French Carmel, is damp and unhealthy, facing onto the sea. Lila stays inside and bakes. Apfelstrudel and kugelhopf and a chocolate wafer cake that hardens in the fridge. Hazelnut cookies dredged in powdered sugar with a dot of strawberry jam. Today, kletzenbrot, a dense fruit bread. It will keep for a long while. She measures and sifts and recombines. Josef has managed to buy sugar beyond the ration on the black market and for this she is glad. She loves baking: the transformation of sugar into caramel, of flour into bread, the frothy exuberance of yeast. Once, years ago, she wanted to study chemistry—a teacher called her talented—but such professions were not possible for girls. Not girls like her, anyway. *La chimie*, chimera.

She really didn't think that the affair with Lev would go on forever, but now that it's over she feels betrayed. Now like the city, she feels hollowed out. The British are mostly gone; seventy thousand Haifa Arabs have fled. Jerusalem is under siege. She's heard that Lev's kibbutz has been attacked. When the war is over, things will no longer be the same. She will wear her knowledge of him like a pearl, a living thing, against her skin, where it will stay lustrous and complete. She feels like a sleeper waking from a dream, as if she's traveled to the outer reaches of the universe without really going anywhere at all. She opens the oven and feels the hot breath in her face, rippling like a wave. She smells the faint reek of gas. She kneels before the oven door, her kidneys, liver, heart, and spleen floating loose inside her body: flotsam, unmoored.

Lila's Story

Near the end of the Mandate, we had to move out from our flat. The British requisitioned it for their troops. We found another one, not so nice as this, down on the French Carmel. You know that I was always crazy for dogs, and one day, my littlest one ran away. You cannot imagine how worried I was! We searched everywhere, calling, calling, but he did not come. Then the next day, there came a knock at the door. It was the landlord, who lived downstairs. Do you have a small white dog? he demanded. Yes, yes! I cried. Have you found him? The landlord said, He ran back to your old flat. The British have him now. You must go to fetch him there. I was afraid, but I had to get my dog back, so I went up to the old flat. The British had retreated to our street with their guns and barbed wire barricades and armored cars. People called these compounds Bevingrads. I was very frightened, but I spoke with the soldiers at the checkpoint and after some discussion they let me through. I went up the steps to our flat and knocked on my own door. An officer answered, holding my little dog in his arms. He was stroking its ears and head. Here you are, Madam, he said, handing the dog to me. I was afraid that he'd be angry with me, but he couldn't have been more kind. Not long afterward, after Independence, we got our own flat back again.

The Book of Life

The married man once wrote me a note that said, Please love me even though you can't have all of me, love me with equanimity. We were in a hotel room, late at night; it was right before the end. I remember seeing my own dilated pupils reflected, huge and black, in the bathroom's mirrored wall; I remember the way my heart felt, beating just a little bit too fast. It isn't true I didn't love him then. When I came back to bed, he took my hands in his and said, Don't believe that I'm the only one. He said, I'm here to show you that men like me exist. He held a mirror up to us and made me look. We were beautiful together, magnificent and grand. Of course, it was nothing but a dream. We made each other up.

My grandmother died a few weeks after that night in the hotel, in the fall, just before Yom Kippur. The Book of Life was open but there was a blank space where her name should have been. I couldn't get to Israel in time for the funeral, which in the Jewish tradition happened the next day. Now, on my last day in Haifa, my uncle takes me down to the cemetery with him. It's at the foot of the Carmel, near the railroad tracks that run along the sea, a dusty narrow space flanked with cypresses. My grandparents are buried beside each other near the end of a long row. I can hear the hum of traffic on the nearby highway to Tel Aviv, the clatter of a passing train, the faint thrum of the sea. Under my grandmother's flat headstone, among decomposing coffin boards and the shredded linen of a shroud, her bones remain. Only a pile of small stones adorns the grave. I bend and place a pebble on the heap to show that I was there.

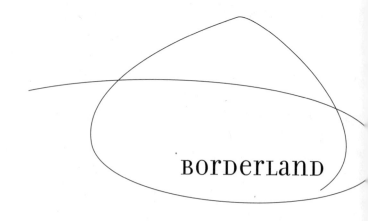

BORDERLAND

Susan could spot an Israeli anywhere. Among the tourists in the Thamel Backpacker's Café—the familiar crowd of Germans and Australians, rangy kids and rugged types who looked ready to head up Everest at a sprint—he stood out right away: the ropy muscles, the jiggling knee, the ashtray full of cigarettes smoked down to the filter or stubbed out half-done. He had broad sideburns, an Adam's apple as sharp as a stone. He was wearing a Nirvana T-shirt and baggy Bedouin pants. He was writing in a notebook. Not left to right.

Two tables over, he looked up. His left eye twitched, then widened—a tic, not a wink. She could walk over and say Shalom, but then she'd be stuck explaining that she didn't really speak Hebrew after all. She could ask him for a cigarette, but she didn't smoke. She could say, My parents are Israeli, too.

From here in the center of town, you couldn't see the mountains, just the white disk of the sun burning through the morning haze. There was a musky scent of incense and donkey dung, a chaos of passing motorbikes and rickshaws, bicycles and beat-up cars, bells and horns and shouts. Across the road, a little girl peeked around the doorway of a child-sized shrine. A dog lay panting in the shade of a stand stacked with bins of mangoes, persimmons, apples, packages of crackers, chocolate bars, wooden flutes, garlands of orange marigolds, bright pink sweets. An old woman squatted by the shop, spat on the dusty ground.

Susan touched the face of her grandmother's watch and counted back. It was nine hours and forty-five minutes earlier back home—still the day before: October 19, 1998. The extra fifteen minutes off New Delhi time were Nepal's little hat-tip of independence from its big neighbors to the north and south—an interval intended, Susan supposed, solely to annoy, or to make you stop and think. She fingered the watch's gold bracelet, its delicate safety chain. She should have left it at home.

In Gaza, the Arabs lined up at dawn. They waited at the checkpoint in taxis, crammed four across the back, in cars and trucks. The heat swirled in a yellow haze. Everywhere, there was sand. The soldiers—Dubi, Ofer, Sergei, Assaf, and the rest of the unit—stood by the concrete barriers and sandbags and razor wire and checked identity cards and waved a metal detector wand. The Arabs were laborers, field hands, merchants, factory workers, students, fishermen. They were on their way to Khan Yunis or Gaza City or across the border to Israel. They carried their belongings in plastic sacks. The women wore loose dresses, scarves wrapped around their heads. They smelled of sweat and cigarettes; their speech tumbled from their throats—glottal ayins, rolling rs. The sea was less than half a mile away. At night, you could hear it breathe.

Go take a hike, Susan's brothers used to say. After a while, her mother started saying it, too, although coming from her, like many English idioms, it never sounded right. She had a way of making everything seem literal. Go take a hike, she'd say, as if she really expected you to jump up, grab your rucksack and alpenstock and march down eight flights of stairs, out into Van Cortlandt Park and across the Bronx.

Susan's grandparents had been the hikers, the lovers of Alpine forests, wildflower glades. Her own parents preferred the beach. What Susan remembered, though, about their summers in Haifa or at the Jersey shore, was that the beach was the place her parents fought. They fought at night, after Susan and her brothers were in bed. They argued in Hebrew, an escalation of harsh whispers breaking through to shouts. Then the screen door would rasp and slam, and Susan would lie awake, anxiety fluttering in her chest, waiting for whoever had gone out to return, but all she ever heard, before she fell asleep, was the hissing of the waves along the shore.

In the morning, of course, she'd find her mother in the kitchen making breakfast as usual, a kibbutznik's bucket cap atop her head, her father drinking his coffee, rustling the newspaper, as he always did, as if nothing at all had happened between them the night before.

It's good to have a short memory, her mother always said, flicking her hands.

But Susan didn't have a short memory. She had a fickle, sticky memory, an inability to let go. She accumulated arguments, misunderstandings, fallings-out and fights, storing them away like the stacks of old letters and photographs she kept in shoe boxes underneath her bed, like her closets full of poorly fitting clothes. Her mother couldn't understand why Susan wouldn't throw things out. Leah was always shedding her own belongings, passing them along—*here, take this Suzi, this is for you*. As a result, nothing got thrown away at all, but piled up at Susan's place instead.

Susan's mother would have liked it here in Kathmandu. She had an enthusiasm for spicy food, exotic scenery, the romance of the East. She loved bargaining for trinkets, the whole charade of feigning outrage and pretending to walk away over the equivalent of fifty cents. She would have made a pilgrimage to every temple, drank the yak butter tea. Susan had actually considered inviting her mother to come along. But when she'd mentioned the trek, Leah had tapped her temple with one finger and said: *At meshuga?* Are you insane? For what do you want to sleep on the ground in the freezing cold? To see some mountains? Go to Switzerland if you want mountains! There at least you can sleep in a bed like a civilized person!

Civilization had its limits, in her mother's mind.

Gaza was a cesspool, and Dubi was the operator of the valve. He turned the spigot on and off. Green light on. Red light off. When the light turned red, the Arabs in their trucks and cars and yellow taxis stopped and sat and waited for the road to open again. They rolled down their windows and fanned themselves with sheets of cardboard or a scarf. They stepped out into the sun or squatted in the shade of the trucks and smoked. Pallets of dahlias wilted in the heat. There was a smell of rotting fish. Cell phones bleeped, babies wailed, chickens clucked, arguments broke out. *Khalas!* the Arabs yelled, waving their fists. Enough.

In the heat of the day, Dubi draped a shirt over the back of his helmet to shade his neck. His M16 rocked against his side like an extra limb, his flak vest heavy and far too hot. He scanned exit permits and searched the trunks of cars. From time to time, he'd pull aside a suspicious man or boy, force him to the ground, and hold him there beneath his pointed gun until a jeep arrived to take him off to jail. But the mid-1990s were not a time of war; from Rabin's assassination in 1995 until the second intifada began, things were relatively quiet there. Quietly, the shit flowed out at dawn, and at dusk it flowed back in again.

The group that Susan had signed up with for the Everest Base Camp trek included a truck driver, a retired shrink, a mining engineer from the Yukon, a neurosurgeon and his wife, a hairdresser from Redondo Beach, and four other single women, all from New York. They stood around the lobby of their hotel, looking, with their baseball caps and fanny packs and camera gear, just like the American tourists that they were. They shook hands and said, Hey, how's it going. Susan wished she had the nerve to travel on her own.

Susan was assigned to share a tent with one of the other single women, who, it turned out, lived only three blocks away from her on the Upper West Side. Joyce was a talkative woman in her mid-thirties with ash-blond hair and a pale, moist face. She'd come on the trip, she told Susan, in hopes of meeting a man, but had already ruled out the immediate possibilities: the truck driver, the hairdresser, the mining engineer. She should have been born a Hindu, she said. An arranged marriage wouldn't be so bad.

Clipboard in hand, the group leader circled around, inspecting their duffel bags and gear. He checked off the essential items, fingered their mummy bags, their water bottles, their stashes of granola bars. When it was Susan's turn, he shook his head. He told her to go rent some fleece pants and a warmer jacket in the Kathmandu bazaar.

Susan skipped the bus tour of Patan and Bhaktapur and headed out to Durbar Square alone. She felt sealed inside her body, her limbs unnaturally light. It might have been the jet lag, although she'd never felt more wide-awake. It was festival time, and the city streets were hung with strings of flowers and prayer flags and tiny lights. Groups of children passed playing flutes and drums, chanting Tihar songs. A girl who could be no more than eleven or twelve carried an infant in a sling across her back, her eyes rimmed in black, her mouth and cheeks smeared red with rouge. Shop windows were stacked with Nikes and Nintendo cartridges, bootleg Chinese CDs and videotapes. In front of the Kathmandu Tours and Travel Agency stood a ribby, sway-backed cow.

In the maze of stalls in the bazaar, Susan found a pair of Russian army-issue fleece pants and a puffy blue down parka that looked as if it had survived its share of Everest expeditions. Feathers flew out of the seams when she pressed on it; it would certainly be warm. She hoped she'd have time to wash the pants before they left for the mountains in the morning. She didn't even want to think about some soldier's unwashed groin.

She was on her way back to the hotel when she noticed him, crouching in the shadow of a courtyard, pointing a video camera at a balcony above. There could be no mistaking those Bedouin pants, that close-cropped hair. Three young monks were leaning over the rail, shiny-headed and bare-shouldered in their saffron robes, jostling each other and waving down to passersby. Susan wondered if this was the Temple of the Living Goddess, the Kumari Devi, the little girl selected by augury, whose feet must never touch the ground. She'd read that the girl sometimes came out onto her balcony, but if this was in fact her home, there was no sign of her now. Susan watched the monks, wondering if they knew they were being videotaped. Didn't they care? She turned around, but the Israeli guy had disappeared.

The army was what everybody did. After high school, you went to the army, and when you got out you did your *miluim* for a couple of weeks a year until you got too old. The army was the melting pot. The army was where you made your closest friends. The army was there for you, for life.

As a child, the only thing Dubi could really imagine about being a soldier was the uniform. He pictured himself in the lace-up boots, the olive-green fatigues, an Uzi underneath his arm. He saw himself hitchhiking at the bus stops, his arm held out, his index finger pointing down. Later, he imagined himself carrying out daring raids on the arms-smuggling tunnels in Rafah, or Syrian positions in the Golan. He'd leap through the gun turret of a tank, crawl on his belly through the burning Negev sand. The army made you strong.

Dubi wasn't even born until the mid-1970s, was just a kid during the Lebanon campaign. He remembered the Gulf War, though. He'd never forget waiting with his mother in their apartment building's basement shelter, their gas masks on. They sat on the edge of a cot, listening for the whistle of an approaching SCUD, the tremor of explosion, the wail of ambulances speeding to the scene. He remembered the metallic taste of adrenaline, the expansion inside his chest as he put his arm around his mother, cupped her shoulder in his hand.

Dubi's father had slipped in his military service—a desk job in

Tel Aviv, on account of his bad back—between '68 and '71, when everything was quiet. He was killed in a car accident in Hadera when Dubi was five years old. Dubi often told people that his father had died in a burning tank in Sinai during the Yom Kippur War. He told the lie so often that it seemed that it was true.

The nineteen-seat Royal Nepal Airways Twin Otter took off at 7:28 a.m., banked sharply to the northwest, and rose out over the terraced fields and knobby green hills of the Terai. Susan pressed her forehead to the window, feeling the vibration of the engines inside her head. In the seat next to her, the truck driver was droning on about the engineering qualities of short-landing-strip aircraft, the high standards of the Nepalese Air Force, the good fortune of a cloudless sky, but Susan wasn't listening. She was watching the shadow of their plane flitting across the valley floor. It was ridiculously small, as insubstantial as a fleck of ash.

A murmur ran through the cabin as the Himalayas appeared in the cockpit windscreen, beyond the pilots' upraised hands. The 26,000-foot snowcapped peaks floated across the horizon, looking just like any other mountains, the Rockies or the Alps, until you remembered that the ground they rested on was over 15,000 feet above sea level to begin with, and that they went up from there. Everything was out of scale.

And then they rounded a crenellated ridge, green and steep, and they were there, the Lukla landing strip rising suddenly in front of them, an uphill dirt runway cut into the mountainside. The plane roared, bounced twice, and skidded to a stop just short of a stone wall. They climbed down underneath the wing, ducking their heads, taking deep breaths of the sun-warmed air that smelled of smoke and mud and ice and pine, 9,200 feet high.

Transported, Susan thought, as they pointed out their duffel bags to the Sherpa porters who had gathered to meet them there. Transported, carried off. It was glorious to be plucked up and carried off like Thumbelina on a swallow's wings. To be raised into the air, like the Kumari Devi back in Kathmandu. What a comedown for her, at puberty, to be sent back to the ground.

The trail to Phakding, their first stop, wound past lowland fields of beans, potatoes, radishes and peas, smoky teahouses, children playing in the sun. The dirt path was broad and flat, more a road than a mountain trail. Susan walked alongside Joyce, her daypack bouncing against her shoulders, her hiking boots rubbing a little on her heel. A Nepali girl passed them, whistling, barefoot, two gigantic duffel bags tied onto her back with a rope looped across her forehead. Outside a teahouse, a sign read COKES $1.50, HOT APPLE PAE. A man passed herding a procession of *dzokyos* and yaks. The air rang with the sound of tumbling water. The sun turned red, lost heat, fell behind the ridge. Susan looked up, light-headed, and wondered if it was possible to get motion sickness solely from the spinning of the earth. A vulture wheeled across the sky.

After dark, they sat inside the Phakding trekkers' lodge and Susan played gin rummy in the light of an oil lamp with Ross, the hairdresser from Redondo Beach. A group of children trouped through the smoke-filled room, giggling and tapping on a Tihar drum, passing around a plate for coins. Is Hindu dharma, the tallest one said. Good luck give. Out the window, a translucent moon ducked behind a hidden peak. Shadows fell across the stubble field, studded with blue and orange tents. There was a peal of laughter, a muffled shout. Hebrew? Here? Susan squinted through the fogged-up glass. Yes, Hebrew, she was almost sure. A shadow passed, the low voice of a man.

Yo Susan, Ross said, waving a hand in front of her face. Gin.

Most Fridays, Dubi went home to Tel Aviv for Shabbat. He hitch-hiked from the border or took the Egged bus. He carried a duffel bag stuffed with dirty laundry and his gun. When he could, he sat on the left side of the bus so he could watch the sun set into the sea. He'd count the seconds it took for it to slide behind the band of haze, flattening as if it were being squeezed beneath an enormous weight of sky. Faster than it seemed possible the earth could turn, the orange sphere would extrude itself into a liquid line, and then the sky and sea would turn dull and flat and it would be gone.

Dubi came home from his week in Gaza like a worker coming home from the factory or fields. He'd climb the steps of his apartment building, ring the doorbell as he fished in his pocket for his key. The bell chirped like a manic bird. Inside, he'd drop his bag, prop his м16 next to the door, call out that he was home. Usually his mother's boyfriend would be there, watching tv, drinking a Maccabi beer out of a can. He was a peacenik, a grizzled hippy type. Oh ho, here comes the big hero, he liked to say.

Dubi ached for home all week but once he got there everything felt wrong. He'd pull off his uniform, take a shower, but it made no difference at all. He couldn't bear his mother's anecdotes about her job at the insurance agency, couldn't care less about what was up with her boyfriend's snot-nosed kids. In the background, the baritone tv newscaster pronounced the word *Gaza* as if it were an outpost on the moon. But Gaza stuck to Dubi, got inside the creases of his skin like sand.

On summer Saturdays, Dubi went with his girlfriend, Maya, to the beach. They spread their towels on the sand. Maya was in the army, too. Her job was showing schoolchildren how to use gas masks. She was a skinny, large-boned girl with a halo of frizzy blondish hair, and she wore a too-short army skirt that gave Dubi a hard-on when he saw her in it, every time. But when she leaned her head against his shoulder, Dubi retracted like a snail. All along the beach, people laughed and played. They whacked racquet balls back and forth, dove into the waves, rubbed suntan lotion on their skin. Gaza was barely seventy kilometers away.

Susan spotted him again just past the crest of the steep hill along the trail to Namche, where the first glimpse of Everest hovered through the trees. He was sitting on a rock, playing a wooden flute. A small crowd of trekkers had gathered there to rest, snap photographs, buy cups of *kala chia* and bottles of Coke from the tea tent set up near the scenic overlook. He hopped down to the ground and picked up his pack as she drew near, fell into step alongside her on the trail. He had on the Bedouin pants again, a baseball cap, cheap Chinese sneakers on his feet. The muscle twitched beneath his eye as his jaw tensed. Not a wink.

Maybe I know you from someplace? he said.

Where are you from? she said, even though she knew.

He told her he was from Tel Aviv, that everybody called him Dubi although his real name was Dov, and that Dov meant "bear." He'd gotten out of the army just before coming to Nepal. He spoke in such a low tone that she had to strain to hear. She couldn't have said what it was, but there was something about him—that nervous energy, or that guttural accent, so like her cousin Gavi's, or the nakedness of the pale skin around his eyes that showed when he pushed his sunglasses up on his head—that kept her walking with him all that afternoon.

The sun was already fading when they rounded the bend to Namche Bazaar, with its terraced fields and red-roofed Sherpa houses built along the curved slope of the cirque. Dubi stopped to light a cigarette, cupping the flame between his hands. Strings of prayer flags fluttered along the houses' eaves, the words of the Buddhist mantra shaking loose and flying out onto the wind. *Om Mani Padme Hum.* Up the hillside, in a stone-walled field next to a whitewashed house, Susan could see the Sherpas setting up their tents. She could hear the sound of singing, women's voices, high and clear. They were praying to Yama Raj, god of the underworld, for the long life of their brothers. It was the last night of Tihar.

Susan's parents' founding myth was this: that her father had caught one glimpse of her mother—then an NYU coed with long dark hair—and followed her around for the next year or two—back to Israel, around New York—until she finally gave in and agreed to go out with him. They were a sexy couple; there was no denying that. You could see it in the photographs—in the way her father folded his arm around her mother's waist, in the heavy-lidded, postcoital look in her mother's eyes. Within three months, they were married; seven months later, Susan was born. Not premature.

This myth—that Susan's mother was a flighty spirit whose feet needed to be held to the ground, that with a single glance, her father knew that they were meant to be—persisted, as such myths do, despite the transformations of the years, despite her father's infidelities, her mother's capacity to forgive, their tugs of war and fights. The myth provided roles for them to play: the skittish maiden, the dogged suitor; the one who pulled away, the one who reeled the other back again. It was possible that they stayed to-gether because of the myth—so her mother could believe that she was free to leave, so her father could believe that he was, in fact, the constant one.

Susan sat in the Namche trekkers' lodge, trying to write a letter to her parents that she couldn't mail until she got back to Kathmandu, meaning she'd already be back in New York when it arrived. Their group leader was sitting across the table, flipping through a two-week-old copy of the *International Herald Tribune*, the headphones of Joyce's Discman on his head. *Making love is a mental disease!* he exclaimed suddenly. For a moment, Susan thought he was talking to her, until she realized those were the lyrics to the song.

Clouds were rolling into the cirque and a fine snow had begun to fall. Susan touched the cornrows she'd let Ross braid in her hair since she wouldn't be able to wash it for the next two weeks. Her scalp felt strangely tight. Already it was hard to remember the smell of the subway, the feeling of high heels, the cursor blinking on her computer screen. She'd stopped feeling that she should check her voicemail or listen to the news. It was good to be away.

At first, Dubi and the others—the plodding Assaf, the kibbutznik Ofer, the Russian Sergei with the missing eyetooth—took the checkpoint seriously. They set their jaws beneath their sunglasses, squared their shoulders, shouted commands into their mega-phones, fired warning shots into the air. But it wasn't long before the whole thing began to drive Dubi mad.

Little by little, it became a game, to see what he could make the Arabs do.

Hey, you.

Hand over those cigarettes.

Go on, sing us a song.

Get down on your hands and knees and bray like the ass you are.

No one stopped him. The commander of the unit leaned back in his chair and chewed on a matchstick and laughed, and everyone else laughed, too.

You're meshuga! they said, tapping a finger to their temples. Dubi took it as the compliment it was meant to be.

Gaza was a landscape made of borders: an IDF patrol line, rolls of electrified barbed wire, concrete blocks, a sandbag barricade, a bulldozed field, a concrete post, a road, a trench. Settlers here, Arabs there, the army in between. There, in the borderland, he discovered you could cross the line.

Over the next six days, along the ascending trail to Khunde, Teng-poche, Pangboche, Dingboche, and into the moraine of Everest itself, Dubi kept showing up. He'd appear midmorning along the trail, or at night inside the trekkers' lodge in the hamlet where they'd camped. He slept in the lodge bunkrooms, ate the teahouse fare, drank the arrack *raksi* and the moonshine *chang*. He gave Susan a hard time about her cushy tent and catered meals. He said, How can you stand being waited on by the fucking Sherpas? They smile too much.

He made her laugh.

Each morning he said, So tell me something new, Suzy Q.

So she told him about the characters in her group: the truck driver's adventures trying to retrieve his glove that fell into a fetid *charpi* pit; the skull (human? monkey? yeti?) that the retired shrink bought from an old woman outside a village *gompa*; how one of the single girls developed acute mountain sickness at twelve thousand feet and had to be carried back to Lukla in a basket on their sardar's back. She told him about her family in Israel, about her cousin Gavi and how close they once had been. She answered his blunt questions (So why don't you come to live in Israel? Why aren't you married? Don't you want to have any kids?) and gave him daily plot updates from *Anna Karenina*, the one book she'd brought along on the trip. She never would have guessed that he'd take an interest in a literary Russian novel, but he was always eager to find out what had happened in the chapters she'd read the night before, as if they were episodes of a soap opera he'd missed. He couldn't get over that Karenin wouldn't give Anna a divorce, or that Vronsky would try to kill himself for love. Russians, he said dismissively. Such people he could not understand.

He told her about his girlfriend, about his mother and her latest man, about his dead father (the tank hero from the Sinai war). He told her he'd like to be a graphic designer, or a film director, or a high-tech entrepreneur. Sometimes he said he'd like to live in California for a while, learn to surf. Other times he said he'd never leave Israel, that all those Israelis living in the States, the *yoredim*, were copping out. She found his twitchy intensity compelling in a way she couldn't quite explain. Mostly, he struck her as being very young.

He's got a major crush on you, Joyce said.

They were arranging themselves for the night, tucking water bottles and contact lens cases deep into their sleeping bags so they wouldn't freeze, pulling on extra long underwear and their night-time hats. It had been days since they'd taken off all their clothes.

Oh come on, Susan said. She checked the clasp on her watch,

then snapped off her headlamp and pulled her mummy bag up around her face. She said, He's just a typical Israeli guy.

Well, Joyce said, he's cute.

Just that day, Susan and Dubi had been the first to arrive at a field where the Sherpas were setting out their lunch. They lay down on a tarp in the hot sun. A milk-green river flowed nearby, a string of spinning prayer wheels suspended in the stream. Out flowed the mantra, burbling on the rushing water: *Om Mani Padme Hum*. There were the sinuous muscles of his arms. There was the smooth skin along the side of his neck. The sun pulsed red behind her eyelids. The edges of their fingers touched. In the roiling green water, the prayer wheels whirled.

Souvenirs. That was the joke—they were collecting souvenirs. A watch. A pack of cigarettes. A photograph.

Ofer had the Polaroid. He took the picture of Dubi with the bloody Arab. The image was overexposed, so that even then, watching his own ghostly body emerge out of the Gaza haze, it already looked like a memory.

Right off, Dubi hadn't liked the look of him—those obsequious cow eyes, those cheeks all graying stubble topped with greasy hair. Put your arms up, Dubi said, and when the Arab did, Dubi hit him, hard. He felt his fist connect with bone, pain radiating through his knuckles, up his arm. The Arab stumbled backward and collapsed onto the road. Dubi cuffed his hands behind his back. Blood was running from the Arab's nose and he was making a low, whimpering sort of sound. When Dubi pulled the Arab up, the blue cloth of the man's jacket clenched in his throbbing hand, Ofer had the camera out and was pointing it at him.

Smile, he said.

When they got back to the post, everyone said what crazy fuckers they were. The truth was he felt happy then. He felt strong.

At Dingboche, 15,200 feet above sea level, Susan lay on her stomach inside her sleeping bag and tried to read. Anna had just told Vronsky that she was pregnant with his child. Levin was droning on about the beauties of a simple life on the land. Susan couldn't concentrate. She had a pounding altitude headache, the communal cough and runny nose. Even with her Russian soldier's fleece pants and the down jacket on over all her other clothes, she was cold. They were above tree level now, on a rubble-strewn plateau left by the glacier's retreating path. Ama Dablam was behind them and Everest dead ahead, a wisp of cloud snagged across its windy peak. Somewhere up there, people were inching their way across the ridge. Susan would never survive an expedition like that. She'd give anything for a shower, a real bed.

It was too dark to read. Susan crawled out of her sleeping bag and pushed back her tent flap to the cold. She could hear the others coughing, the barking of a dog. Suddenly, Lhotse appeared from behind a snake of cloud, its snowy flank gleaming golden-pink as if lit from within. Then in a swirl of wind, the vision disappeared. She could see why people invested mountains with mystical belief.

In the *thangka* paintings inside every village *gompa*, the Sakyamuni Buddha pointed to the ground, calling the earth to witness. The monks blew horns carved from human femurs. Here we are. See.

The light was almost gone. In front of the tents, Ross stood juggling limes borrowed from the cook. A group of dirty-faced children had gathered around to watch. In down overalls and a multipocket vest, his curly hair sticking out from under a knit cap pulled low over his brows, Ross looked like a ragged jester holding court. The limes flew up in a circle, over his head and around. The children laughed. *Ooooh, dai!* they cheered.

Inside the teahouse, a Sherpa girl was cooking rice and dal, while an old woman rocked an infant in a cradle on the floor. The yak-dung fire threw off a choking smoke into the chimneyless room, but at least it was fairly warm. The old woman rocked the cradle with her foot, rapidly back and forth, back and forth, in time to her muttered mantra. *Om Mani Padme Hum.* The grandmother looked ancient, hunched and lined, but the girl was surely no more than twenty and the baby just a few weeks old. How could anyone give birth in such a place, a six-day walk from anywhere? They were light-years from the sun, on a rocky, ice-bound moon.

He wasn't the only one.

When the Arab dropped his identity card, Sergei made him crawl after it in the dirt and then kicked him in the head.

Ofer posed two men naked in front of their wives and kids and took their photograph while the rest of the soldiers stood around and jeered.

Assaf let the one-armed merchant cross, but without his donkey cart. Today only one asshole gets through, he said.

They found ways to close the road and keep them waiting at the checkpoint for hours so they'd miss a day of work. They let through the old man who said he needed dialysis, but turned away the pregnant girl. They shot at the little boys who hurled stones at them from behind the concrete barricades. They said, That's the only way they'll learn.

They were average soldiers, average kids. They did the things they did because they could.

Now, here in Nepal, Dubi watched the trekkers—the young Americans and Australians and Japanese and Brits—partying in the teahouses late at night. On his way outside, he stepped over the Sherpa guides and porters who lay sleeping, curled up with the dogs, like dogs themselves, outside on the ground.

He watched them posing together along the trail, in front of tilted mani stones and snowy mountain backdrops, the trekkers and their Sherpa guides, arm in arm. He willed his body not to tense up as he watched them smile.

It came on in the middle of the night: stomach cramps, nausea, the runs. Susan stumbled to the latrine, clutching her jacket closed against the wind. Inside, her headlamp illuminated clumps of soiled toilet paper littered around the feces-smeared hole. She retched. Somewhere, not far away, a dogfight erupted into snarls. Back in the tent, Joyce slept, her breathing ragged in the oxygen-poor air, her mummy bag cinched around her face. Susan fought the urge to wake Joyce up. She lay feverish and shivering in the dark, listening to the rattle of the tent zippers in the wind.

At dawn, the group leader stuck his fur-covered head under the flap and touched her leg. Are you coming? he said. They were getting an alpine start on the climb to Kala Pattar, the black peak overlooking Everest, the Khumbu icefall and base camp. Today was the high point of the trip.

She could hear the others outside the tent, the sounds of Velcro and people spitting and stomping their feet on the frozen ground.

No, go on, she said, I'll just wait here for you all to get back.

She sipped some water from her Nalgene bottle, dizzy, and lay down again. The world had shrunk to the confines of this triangular burrow, this ripstop nylon sky.

Once, as a little girl, she'd gotten lost. They were in the transit lounge at Heathrow Airport, en route to Tel Aviv. Susan remembered waiting in a shop by a revolving rack of books. Her mother stood off to one side. She wore a light blue thigh-length coat. Susan followed the coat around the rack and across the lounge. She reached for the light blue hem—a pinwale corduroy—and held on. But when she looked up, there was a strange woman peering down at her, her eyes empty and surprised. Susan let go and the room tipped, the air squeezed from her lungs. There was an ocean of orange and blue carpet, a forest of bucket seats bolted to the floor. Outside the enormous plate glass windows, jets lifted off into the glare. Susan didn't remember the voice over the loudspeaker calling her name. There must have been shouting and tears, the smother of an embrace, but she didn't remember any of that. She didn't remember being found.

Here on the black shale crest of Kala Pattar, looking out onto the white sea of peaks that marked the border with Tibet, Dubi felt the energy rising like a snake. It rose through his chakras, from the root of his perineum to his head, with a burst of color and a receding rush of heat, like the Kabbalist Sefirot emanating from the void. Each chakra was a spinning lotus blossom wheel. The vibration quickened, his body aligning to true pitch. He was trembling, his tongue thick inside his mouth, a cracking sound inside his head. He was disintegrating into particles of light.

When he opened his eyes again, everything was clear.

When Dubi entered the Lobuche trekker's hut at midday, Susan's first thought was that he looked stoned—his pupils dilated, his eyes a little strange—but it could have just been the effect of coming indoors from the glare. She felt a rush at the sight of him. He was the first familiar face, other than their Sherpa cook, that she'd seen since dawn. When he sat down on the bench beside her, she held out her arms. He reached forward, pulling her against him so close that she could feel the thumping of his heart. He held her that way for so long that she had to disengage to breathe. She pushed back, but hung onto his arms. She felt that she would float away without him there to keep her on the ground. Despite her queasiness, despite the cold, she longed to feel his skin on hers. The weakness in her knees wasn't only from the stomach bug.

He was looking at her hard, the suntan lines around his eyes amplifying his stare. For a split second she had the strange impression that he was about to cry. But then his left eye twitched, his jaw contracted, and he looked away, patting down his pockets for his pack of cigarettes.

She knew then that Joyce was right. Here she was in three layers of unwashed clothes, a bandanna tied around her greasy cornrowed hair, her legs as hairy as a guy's, and he was looking at her that way. It wasn't a familiar sensation. Usually she was the one knocked off balance by romance.

It was only noon. Joyce and the others wouldn't be back for hours. Why shouldn't she do exactly what she wanted for once?

Hey, she said, reaching under the table for his hand. Come with me.

After Lobuche, everything changed.

The colors of the landscape grew more intense. Dubi could feel the music of his muscles and ligaments and joints, the swirling flows of blood and lymph and air. He could feel the harmony of the wind and stones and rustling trees, the vibration of the sunshine and the scudding clouds. He listened to the backbeat of his heart.

In Pangboche, he sat with the monks inside the *gompa* and watched them meditate. The Buddha smiled down at him in end-less repetition from the walls, his thumb and middle finger pressed together, a swirl of blue and orange and green. Dubi took it as a sign. There was the drone of chanting, the chesty vibration of the gong, the clear tone of a silver bell. Afterward, outside the *gompa*, the letters carved into the mani stones floated loose and rearranged themselves before his eyes.

Dubi knew that what happened to him on Kala Pattar was real and not just another magic mushroom trip. Along the trail back down to Lukla, it came to him in little bursts, like flashes of white light.

After Lobuche, even though there was still a week left to the trek, every step was a return. They walked back the way they came, head-ing down through Pangboche, Tengboche, Namche, the names a musical refrain—*going home, going home*. The fact that the way was now imaginable changed everything. The intensity of the alpen-glow on a drifting peak, the mysticism of red-robed monks, the tableaux of Sherpa women digging roots out of the frozen fields had faded to the merely picturesque. They were sick of coughing and spitting, of dirty fingers and the runs, of the cold and dust and yak dung everywhere. They'd be home before Thanksgiving. They wanted hot showers, clean hair, a bed with sheets and a pillow, a newspaper, TV.

Namche Bazaar, with its whitewashed houses, electric light, trekkers' lodges, and street-side shops, felt like civilization now. They wandered through the crowds on market day, taking pictures of the Tibetans who'd come over the pass to trade meat and salt. The Tibetans wore rough sheepskin outfits and high felt boots, black braids wrapped around their heads and tied with bits of red cloth. They shopped for souvenirs: turquoise rings, woven carpets, *thangkas*, beaded bracelets, yak-wool sweaters, fur-trimmed embroidered hats. They waved to the smiling Sherpa girls, calling out *Namasté, didi!* the way the locals did. Susan took off her Russian soldier's pants and put on jeans. They were loose now at the waist, a good sign.

With Dubi, there was a studied effort on both their parts to behave as if everything was still the same—overly casual greetings and good-byes, a friction as their eyes met and shifted away. His feint of distance filled her with a delicate desire. At night, in the darkness of her tent, she replayed their afternoon together like a tape. The roughness of his tongue. The flex of muscles, the circle of his arms.

After Gaza, in those long weeks before he'd left for the Far East, all he'd done was sleep. He went to bed early and slept until noon. He slept with his pillow pressed over his head to block out sound. In the afternoons, he sat by the swimming pool at the Hilton, where Maya had a job, watched the tourists waddle past. His head felt dense as cotton wool. Even the air felt particulate, as if it had condensed to sand.

But now Dubi couldn't sleep. His eyes refused to close. His body cast a long shadow as he walked along the streets of Namche in the light of the full moon. He was gigantic, taller than the houses, taller than the trees.

He could see it clearly, the way things would be. He understood that everything up to now had been a trial, preparing him for this.

Back in Kathmandu at last, Susan shed the trek along with her smelly clothes. She stood under the shower for half an hour, letting the hot water flood her eyes and lips. Then Ross came to her hotel room with his scissors and trimmed six inches off her hair. Crescents of hair covered the bathroom floor.

Susan put on sandals and a sleeveless dress. Her hair swung against her neck. She sat down on the bed and turned the TV on to CNN. The stock market was still going up. Impeachment hearings for the president had begun. *Armageddon* was a huge box office hit. She hadn't thought about the news in days.

Dubi was standing in the lobby when she came downstairs. He hadn't showered or changed, and she felt a small shiver of distaste. He was looking at her in that odd way again. The clenched-jaw grimace seemed more pronounced against the stubble of his suntanned face. In two days, she'd be back home. She wished she could have preserved her memory of him the way he was during the trek—a perfect souvenir. But here he was, looking at her like that.

Ooh-ah, he said. You are beautiful.

I was about to go out for a walk, she said. She knew he felt her distance. He was pulling her down, a heavy stone. She could see the pain fracture in his eyes.

He said, I'll come, too.

He reminded her of a boy in her fifth-grade class who used to follow her around, his tongue practically lolling out. He wrote her love notes and made his sister slip them into her desk. At recess, the other boys would beat him up and jeer and he would just lie there in the dirt, his arms and legs curled limply to his chest, until they were done. Come on, guys, don't, he'd whimper. Andrew. That was the boy's name.

Dubi pushed open the door and they stepped out of the air-conditioned lobby chill into the gritty heat. Sea level was a comedown. The smells of diesel exhaust and garbage settled like a weight.

Dubi said nothing as they walked but Susan could tell he was turning words around inside his head. He seemed to have lost his flirty humor, his aggressive Israeli style. In their place was that almost manic energy, those circles beneath his eyes. The image of her cousin Gavi rose in her mind before she could shut it out.

They were crossing a courtyard off Durbar Square when he pulled her to a stop, took her hands in his. She glanced up, over his shoulder, and recognized the balconies of the temple of the Kumari Devi, the same place she'd seen him, videotaping, back at the beginning of it all. The balconies were empty now, the windows reflecting the orange sun.

What he said was not what she expected. She wasn't sure she even understood it all. Something about a message he'd received, a sign. Something about the connection between them, how special she was—far more than she could know.

There is a reason we found each other, he said. It is not just a coincidence.

Coincidence. What was *coincidence*, really, but incidents randomly occupying the same place in space or time? Everything was a co-incidence, if you thought about it that way. The two of them were a case in point. Here they were, holding hands, but they'd never really touched at all.

Still, Susan felt herself softening a little bit. He was just a kid. He'd get over her soon enough. She reached up and kissed him on the cheek. She was feeling generous now.

Who knows, she said. Maybe some day we'll meet again.

B'seder, he said. Okay.

It was not so difficult. Her room was only on the second floor. He swung himself up to the balcony and crouched there in the darkness, listening. Below him, in the hotel garden, hibiscus flowers stretched their stamens up and spread their petals wide. The city's glow dimmed the stars. In the distance came the sound of a motorbike's high whine, the barking of a dog.

He pressed his forehead against the sliding door and let his eyes adjust. There was the dim outline of the bed. An uneven shape on top. He pushed gently against the glass. The door slid open, as he'd known it would.

He felt her before he could see her, the silent rise and fall of breath, the subtle movement of her shoulders, the faint flutter of her eyelids. He inhaled deep into his lungs, timing his own breath to hers. Blood pulsed through his limbs like light.

She turned, flinging an arm above her head, moaning softly in her sleep. The sheet pulled back across her chest; her skin glowed like the moon.

He crouched down, bracing himself against the wall as he slipped the lens cap off, lifted the video camera to his eye, pressed the button. *Record.*

He filmed until the tape ran out. He was so close that he could see the hairs along her bare arms, the soft down along her neck.

It was only then that he noticed the glint of light. It was a watch, round-faced, gold, lying on the night table next to the lamp. The hinged bracelet held in a circle by a chain. He put it to his ear, felt the beating of its tiny heart. Inside his shirt pocket, against his chest, it pulsed with his blood. Outside, a misshapen moon dangled in the sky. The air was warm as skin.

The hotel manager said he could not call the police since there was no sign that her room had been broken into or anything disturbed. Perhaps it has been misplaced, he said. He noted her address and phone number, tucked the paper into the pocket of his shirt. He said, Madam, we will certainly inform you if anything turns up, so Susan knew she'd never hear from him again.

It is not fucking misplaced, Susan told Joyce afterward as they waited for their midnight flight from Delhi to New York to board. My grandmother gave me that watch, Susan said, when I turned thirteen. I knew I should have left it at home.

She felt the thickness of the dark, the breathing of another body too close to hers, the violation of space. She pushed the thought from her mind.

In the windowless Delhi transit lounge, birds were twittering in the branches of an indoor ficus tree. Two lavatory attendants, squatting against the far wall by their buckets and brooms, took turns sipping from a thermos of tea. She rubbed her fingers over the tan line that marked where the watch should have been. Was it now on some Nepali chambermaid's wrist, or in a dusty pawnshop off Durbar Square? She missed its familiar face, its comforting soft tick. It seemed impossible that it was gone.

She closed her eyes and leaned back in the uncomfortable plastic chair. It was a sunny afternoon in a stubble field, prayer wheels spinning in a milky stream. Words were tumbling through the water, blowing through the air. The sun pulsed red against her eyelids. She felt the closeness of another hand beside her own.

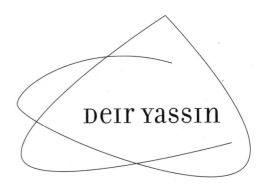

Deir yassin

As Dawn Splits

All the way from New York to Tel Aviv, she keeps the box beneath the seat in front of her. She slips off her sandals and touches it with her toes. A movie flickers overhead; the darkened shades are rimmed with static slits of light. The man next to her guffaws into his headphones. Thirty-six thousand feet up, she's thinking about the many possibilities of return. In a Tibetan air burial, bodies are left naked on a rock for vultures to pick to bones. In India, pyres smolder along the Ganges, ashes and marigolds drifting with the stream. Maybe she'll just leave the box at Ben Gurion, revolving like a planet on a baggage carousel. Maybe she'll drop it inside the Damascus Gate, ticking like a bomb. Or maybe she'll take it to a café deep inside the souk and stir the ashes, a teaspoonful at a time, into a cup of Arabic coffee, boiled sweet. She'll turn the cup over, twist it three times, read the prophecy etched into the grinds. As dawn splits over the Mediterranean, three men in black suits and rumpled shirts shuffle past her and place themselves in the space between the galley and the lavatories, behind her seat. They wind phylacteries around their arms and foreheads, drape prayer shawls over their heads, and daven toward the streaks of light. She feels the chanted words bending, bobbing, against her neck. The words keep the hurtling plane miraculously aloft. Susan touches the box with her toes and listens to the praying men. She's thinking that bodies, like words, dissolve, dry up, fly into the air. They fly away and are gone.

Here Buried

Avraham Bar-On wakes at dawn. As he buttons his shirt, he looks out the window at the Jerusalem pines and flat rooftops of Givat Shaul. The early light is flat and gray. He boils coffee at the stove, tosses yesterday's bread to the pigeons waiting on the windowsill. He is thinking about the town where he was born, pigeons pecking at the cobbled square at dawn, the women setting up their market stalls, their heads wrapped in flowered scarves, squat burlap sacks filled with barley and corn and rye, or in summer, buckets of lilies and gladiolas from the fields. Avraham takes off his glasses, wipes them with a dishrag. He knows these images may not really be memories at all, but just the sediment of stories he's been told, or photographs he's seen in books. He was just a child when he left Poland, and he has never returned. He was Abie Borodsky then, another person in another world. Here, too, beneath his feet, lie other lives, other worlds. Here buried under layers of broken stone and dirt and dust lie, perhaps, some potsherds, a Roman coin, a cistern, abandoned graves. Two thousand years from now, he thinks, everything will still be much the same. The indifferent sun will still appear each day, though little will remain to show that he was ever here—an aluminum can, a splinter of bone. Maybe it's the news of his brother Zalman's death that has done it—lately everything around him has started to recede, as if he were on a banking plane watching the green-brown squares of cultivated earth curve out and slip away. He thinks of his wife, Eva, strapped to her chair in the hospital ward, her memory gone, her mind as blank as air. Avraham doesn't pick up the paper lying outside his door; he doesn't listen to the morning news. He stands by the stove, sipping his coffee, bitter and black, as the light grows sharp over the stones.

A Sky Blue Marble

Susan carries the box containing the ashes of her dead uncle off the plane, through immigration, past the baggage carousels, and out the lane marked NOTHING TO DECLARE, into the light. People push and wave and shout, pressing against the barricades outside the sliding doors. No one is here to greet her. There's the smell of too many bodies, of flesh and sweat. Susan has been to Israel many times, but this time everything looks strange, as if illuminated by a too-bright light. She's struck by the rising cadence of language she does not understand, by the Hebrew letters surrounding her on billboards, blocky and obscure. She notices the soldiers, M16s swinging at their sides, the Mizrahi men with gold chains around their necks, Arab families tugging enormous suitcases on wheels, Haredim in black with side curls at their ears. Almost no tourists.

Susan holds the box on her lap as the *sherut* winds up the road to Jerusalem. She rolls down her window and breathes the hot dry air that smells of diesel exhaust and pine: familiar, foreign smells. A burned-out armored van tilts on the verge, a relic of the first war. New trees line the hillsides, rows of saplings orderly as military graves. She is the last passenger to be dropped off. The driver does not want to take her to East Jerusalem. He lectures her in a Russian-inflected Hebrew, waving his hands and glaring at her in the rearview mirror, from which an amulet swings, a sky blue marble against the evil eye. She makes out the word *intifada*, the words *Aravim* and *Yehudim*, Arabs and Jews. The American Colony Hotel, once a pasha's palace, is a favorite of journalists and diplomats who don't mind its location in the Arab part of town. The lobby is cool and dim, with vaulted arches and floors of time-worn stone. In these troubled times, it is quiet as a tomb. Past the lobby, Susan can see the empty tables in the courtyard café, the Turkish fountain burbling beneath an orange tree. Susan does not give the box to the bellboy who leads her to her room. She carries it before her like a gift, feeling the rasp of sediment shifting inside.

Pigeon

On the morning before the day he died, Zalman Bar-On lay awake behind hazy slats of light and tried to remember his dream. A pigeon had flown in through the bedroom window—although it was not this bedroom, but another one that reminded him of their first apartment in Chicago, the one with the smell of gas in the hallway and a rust-rimmed sink. The pigeon flew in through the window and his ex-wife, Shula, carried the bird out to the fire escape and let it go. It flapped up into the yellow sky and was gone. Then Zalman was alone and he was holding the pigeon on his finger, its knotty talons piercing his skin. The bird led him through the rutted streets of a village both familiar and strange, with old stone houses and olive trees trembling in the rain. The dream annoyed him. He shook it off with the sheets and got out of bed. The floor felt cold underfoot. The water ran cold in the bathroom sink.

The Second Hand

In the flat on Amram Gaon Street the second hand
of Avraham Bar-On's kitchen clock is stuck
between the three and the four. It quivers
and gives out a low hum like a moan
before springing reluctantly ahead.
Avraham has washed his cup and plate
and is trying to decide what to do next.
In the old days, he'd be at the university by now,
his work spread out like a fan inside his head.
But these days, time keeps getting stuck
like this clock, whose batteries
probably need to be replaced.

Patrimony

Susan's room looks out over a too-blue swimming pool, where one lone hotel guest reclines oily in the sun. She sets the box on the table next to the complimentary basket of fruit and stack of glossy tourist magazines, and sits down on the bed. It is her first trip to Jerusalem in years. Now her grandparents are dead; this time it is the other side of the family she has come to see: her mother's oldest brother, Avraham Bar-On, a man she hardly knows. She has brought him the box.

Susan often feels related only to her father. People always say she looks just like her mother, with her thick-lashed eyes and long dark hair, but Susan's good sense of direction, her reporter's desire for the story, her crooked little toe, are all his. Susan's mother has always promoted the myth of Susan's lack of relation to her own family, whose women (she said) were prone to nervous disorders, hypertension, leaky heart valves, and untimely death. Susan's mother had tried to evade her legacy the old-fashioned way, trading one patrimony for another in marriage, but who was to say what she'd passed along to her daughter, this lone girl among brothers and cousins, uncles and sons, and sometimes Susan wondered what weakness lay on her X chromosomes, like a point of metal fatigue on the wing of a plane.

Susan narrows her eyes and considers the box. She tries to imagine the rush of heat—the yellow roar—the residue of bone and ash. She tries to imagine her own body, shadowed behind a screen of flames. She imagines herself as weightless as air, the whisper of release.

Jerusalem Syndrome

Avraham takes his cap and cane and walks south along Amram Gaon Street before turning onto Kanfei Nesharim in the direction of Har Nof. To avoid tripping, he walks in the road, preferring the idea of sudden death beneath a car's wheels to the lingering decline of broken bones. A driver swears out his window, leaning on his horn. Avraham passes a clutch of religious boys from the yeshiva, shouting at each other and scuffing their black shoes in the dust. He passes two small children squatting beneath the broad boughs of a pine, cracking open *snobarim* with a chalky stone. The sun presses white and hot like the palm of a hand. Halfway up the hill, Avraham pauses to rest in the thin shade of a eucalyptus tree. The pavement shimmers in the heat. Just beyond the crest, Avraham knows, is the Kfar Shaul Mental Health Center, a cluster of stone buildings surrounded by a barbed wire fence, an olive grove, pine and almond trees, and heaps of cracked concrete and tumbled stone. Before the battles of 1948, it was an Arab village. Even now, Palestinians still call it Deir Yassin, although it isn't marked on any map. After the war, they built a mental hospital there to care for Holocaust survivors gone mad; now it's where they bring people afflicted with the Jerusalem Syndrome—tourists, usually, found ranting or dressed in robes, claiming to be Elijah or Christ and shouting warnings of the apocalypse. Sometimes, close by the gate, you could hear the false prophets shouting or crying—it was impossible to tell. Avraham himself prefers to look to the past, not the future: his stories run like memory, from back to front, the answers written at the beginning, not the end.

What Zalman Remembered

What Zalman remembered many years later was
a thin disk of sun burning through the ashen sky
the wind out of the Judean hills hissing through the pines
the metallic taste of fear like blood in his mouth
a woman pouring coffee in the cold static time before
the fighting began, talking about the Jews murdered
at Gush Etzion, the thirty-five martyrs of the Lamed-Heh.
The woman said, You give those Arabs something
they'll remember this time.
Zalman remembered the loudspeaker truck

sent to warn the villagers, stuck in a rut
blaring like Cassandra into the flat blank dawn
Evacuate! Evacuate!
but nobody heard.
He remembered low stone houses chickens children Arabs dust
machine gun fire an exploding grenade the boom
of the two-inch mortar sent by the Palmach when the fighting
    turned bad
the smell of burning the shouting the screams
a boy of no more than nine or ten hurling a homemade bomb
an old man cowering, knock-kneed, dressed in a woman's
    clothes.
Later, witnesses said the Jewish fighters' eyes were glazed as if in
    ecstasy,
but Zalman doesn't remember any ecstasy but fear.
Pain, of course, was the one thing that evaded memory—
he remembered only the sensation of falling and later great
    thirst.
The bullet nicked the femur of his left leg
but missed the artery; they gave it to him afterward
in a paper bag. A trophy or a souvenir.
The only thing that still remained
was the scar on the outside of his left thigh,
a pink shiny patch like a small, exploded star.

Evening Bells

In the early evening, Susan phones Avraham from her room. She
sits on the edge of the bed, listening to the clicks as the call goes

through. Six rings before he picks up. *Hallo?* he hollers, as if she must be very far away. It's Leah's daughter, Susan, she says, from the States. *Mi zeh?* he yells. More slowly, she repeats: *Ha bat shel Leah.* Leah's daughter. (How do you say "your niece"? She isn't sure.) Ah yes, he says in English. Of course. A gritty voice, a European not Israeli accent, with a British tinge. In the distance, Susan hears the evening bells: Armenian, Anglican, Latin, Abyssinian, Russian, Greek. The sound radiates like ripples in a pool. You are at a hotel? her uncle says. This I cannot allow. Tomorrow you will come to me. I will fetch you in the morning. No, no, it is impossible. With the situation as it is now. *Ha matzav.* Susan looks out the window. The city is cooling from white to golden-pink in the slanting sun. She has no desire to leave this beautiful hotel. The old man's flat is in that religious neighborhood, Givat Shaul, and almost certainly has no air-conditioning and a cold-water shower or the kind of water heater you have to ignite with a match. It's probably filled with piles of paper, or potsherds—he was an archeologist—and she recalls that his wife has Alzheimer's and is in a home. She thinks of the last time she saw her dead uncle Zalman's apartment in Chicago, with the smell of cooking in the halls, the soot that seeped in at the edges of the window frames. He would offer her hard candies from a bowl, the plastic wrappers glued to peppermints gummy with age. Take, take, he'd insist. And when the woman hadn't come to clean there would be scabs of food on the forks, for he never wore his glasses when he washed the dishes. Now Avraham is going on about how one no longer goes to King George Street or the Jaffa Road. One must not walk alone at night. Do not take the yellow Arab cabs. His warnings annoy her, though they make her wonder how much things really have changed since she last was here, before the Al-

Aqsa intifada began. Even her parents said she was crazy to come.
Still. She will hand over the box and be done.

Words

Because her Hebrew is not good, in Israel Susan's always a tourist,
or if not exactly a tourist, someone who can't exactly pass
for a sabra, even though this is the place her family is from,
or if not exactly from, the closest thing to it
(closer anyway than New York or Berlin or Vienna or Lwów).
Everyone speaks English here in any case, and even if not, Susan
    can usually get by
in her limping Hebrew restricted to a few dozen nouns and the
    present tense.
It's a troublesome language that Eliezer Ben-Yehuda resurrected
from biblical ossification with its absence of vowels and no verb
    "to be."
The sequence of consonants *gimel*, *lamed*, and *shin*, Susan knows,
    can be read as
golesh (to overflow like hot frothy milk or streaming wet hair),
or as its opposite, *gelesh* (baldness),
or even as *le-haglish* (to publish, in the sense of words flowing to
    light, like the skin on a newly bald scalp).
The root *gimel-lamed-shin* also forms the words *maglesha*,
    miglasha, *miglashayim*, *gilshon*, *gelisha*:
a slide, a sled, a pair of skis, a surfer, a hang glider, an avalanche.
The way letters slip around it's not surprising that the Kabbalists
    tried to shake loose
the letters of God's very name from their usual signification,
as if meaning itself could overflow and slip away

like a pot boiling over, wet hair fanning out in a pool, a sparkler's
   shower of light.

Where Her Blood Jangles

Now she's sitting in the cellar bar twisting the stem of her wine
glass between her forefinger and thumb, feeling that strange way
you feel sometimes when you travel alone—an echoing inside your
head as if the words in there have no place to go but just bump
around like a bluebottle fly on a windowpane. Two fair-haired men
are sitting at a table in the corner, speaking some lilting language,
Swedish perhaps, eating roasted peanuts out of their palms. The
bartender is a young fellow with jutting elbows and eyebrows that
meet in an arc at the bridge of his nose and skin pockmarked like
orange rind. He refills her glass, not quite looking at her but not
quite looking away, and when she thanks him, he says: Please. He
could be an Israeli Arab or a Mizrahi Jew or a Druze: he has features
she can't read. Susan herself is the kind of person to whom people
sometimes say, But you don't look Jewish! She has long, straight
hair, amber-flecked eyes, a nose that tapers to a bump. The truth
is that inside, where her blood jangles and her breath beats against
her ears, she doesn't exactly feel Jewish either. She feels hollow,
like a knotty gourd.

Night Sounds

Avraham sits on the terrace and listens to the night sounds in the
   dark—
engines revving at the stoplight, a cat wailing like a colicky child,
the drone of the nine o'clock news on someone's TV.
The economic outlook's even worse. Tomorrow, hot, khamsin.

But right now it's cool—he's wrapped himself in a shawl like an old
　　woman
and is listening to the cicadas' creak. Someone is shouting—Avi
　　Avi—a mother
calling for her child to come in. So once his mother called to him,
　　too—Avi Avi—
as dusk dropped over the bald hills. He remembers racing

up the three stone steps from the garden, slippery with pine
　　needles,
the smells of thistles, goat dung, apricots rotting on the rocky
　　ground.
There were still jackals in the wadi then, hyenas, too. It doesn't
　　seem possible
that breathless boy in khaki shorts could really have been him.

He has never thought much of Freud's interest in archeology,
his likening of the tumbled ruins of the past to the unconscious
　　mind,
as if memory were something you could excavate, analyze, piece
　　together, solve,
instead of a story you invent in the shape of your desire.

Take his brother Zalman, that other phantom boy he hasn't seen in
　　years.
Lately he's begun to confuse Zalman in his memory with their
　　father.
He sees them both as bearded old men with cloudy eyes, bent like
　　Polish rabbis

over Torah scrolls. Only his father was the religious one, not
    Zalman.
Zalman was a different kind of zealot. A patriot. A pioneer. He
    remembers
his father and Zalman arguing, hardheaded, at the kitchen table
    in the old flat
in Sanhedria, after Zalman told them he was joining the Irgun.
    Those terrorists?
their father yelled. The bread knife jumped. Or has he made this
    memory up, too?

Zalman Wondered

Near the end, Zalman wondered how it was that he was still here,
here in America, in this place he'd only intended to stay a year or
two or five at most, until the situation back home, the flap over the
Irgun, settled down. It was Shula who suggested it, who wrote to
her cousin in the wonderful-sounding Champaign, Illinois. Just
for a year or two, they said. Then we'll see. They took only three
suitcases and left the cat behind, that odd gray cat with yellow eyes
that vanished, they found out later, on the very day they decided
to stay on in the States another year. Cats know things, Shula said.
She was mystical about animals, though not about much else. He
himself kept half-expecting that cat to turn up one day in Chicago,
having followed them there the way pets sometimes did. He'd find
himself peering behind the trashcans in the alley, listening for
her cry at night. Eventually, they took in a stray instead, a blind
old tabby with one torn ear. Now the cat and Shula both were gone,
and here he was still. But never for a moment had he meant to stay

for good. Even now, whenever he said home, he still always meant there.

Here

At 2:17 a.m. she opens her eyes, wide awake.
For a moment the bed tilts, the grainy darkness swirls.
The door and the window have changed places.
Then she remembers. Here she is. Here.
She remembers a night when she was eight or nine or ten,
lying awake in a hard unfamiliar darkness
her first night in a flat rented for the summer
with a strange stretched feeling at the back of her throat
like the memory of a yawn that wouldn't come.
She remembers running in a panic barefoot
across the cold floor to her parents' room,
and her mother soft and dozy in her loose nightgown
giving her a glass of milk and a quarter of a Darvon
to help her sleep. Here take this. Here.
She remembers once her brothers and cousins,
digging in the garden behind her grandparents' flat,
turned up beneath the stony dirt the skeleton
of a cat. Maggots had left the bones bright and clean.
There was a one-legged Russian, their grandmother said,
who lived next door and kept two dozen cats. At night they'd
     scream
like infants in pain. He fed them fish heads from a canvas bag,
stumping on his wooden peg. He died maybe ten years ago,
she said, and the cats ran off, thank G-d. Good riddance to
     them all.

The boys covered the bones with fresh dirt and said kaddish
for the cat. They said, *Yitgadal v'yitkadash sh'meyh rabbah*.
There sits the box, heavy-gauge cardboard
labeled CREMATED REMAINS. Cremations are forbidden
here. The Orthodox say the body belongs to God alone,
that this spinning world is neither the beginning
nor the end of man. So what remains? Nothing.
She believes nothing, and yet here she is,
carrying out a dead man's will. Maybe the word
for it is just *nostalgia*.
She's starting to feel a little sleepy again. She turns
the pillow over to the cool side. Now sleep.

He Who Has Spent His Life Digging

Avraham, having fallen asleep in his chair on the terrace, wakes
at exactly 2:17 a.m. according to the kitchen clock (which might
or might not still be stopped or running slow) and stumbles in
to bed. The breeze has died and the air is still and dense as sand.
He switches off the light and as he lies back he tries to imagine
what it would be like to be buried alive, the weight on his chest,
the pressure in his lungs, the smothering blackness the same with
your eyes open or closed. He opens and closes his eyes now and,
perceiving no difference, wonders if he's suddenly gone blind.
But slowly the outline of the wardrobe floats toward him, then the
faint stripes of the blinds. He thinks of Zalman. Fifty years he's
been away and now he wants his ashes scattered here. His ashes!
Leave it to Zalman to desire such an outrageous thing. It is fitting,
he supposes, that he, Avraham, who has spent his life digging dead
things out of the ground, should now be the one to add another

body to this necropolis Jerusalem. But where? In the parklands of Hinnom, where the Canaanites sacrificed their children to the gods? On Ha-Ofel, by the Jebusite graves or the false tomb of Absalom? Or right here in the cemetery in Givat Shaul? Avraham feels a certain chill at the thought of Zalman's ashes mingling with the nearby dead of Deir Yassin. I told that boy not to join those bandits the Irgun, their father had said when the telephone call came to say that Zalman had been shot. Bloody terrorists, he said, spitting over his shoulder, *pthew, pthew*, when they heard that open carts of Arab prisoners from the village had been paraded down King George V Street before a cheering crowd. Later, they heard other stories, too, that the Arabs were taken to a quarry behind the village and shot—a hundred or two hundred or even more. They tried to bury the story, but there were those who remembered still. Those who saw. Their frozen eyes. Their blood-stained clothes.

Khamsin

Khamsin is the Arabic word for fifty:
the fifty days of hot wind from the east
blowing dust and grit through a yellow sky
like a last exhalation of exhaust
out of the throat of the Sahara sphinx.
The old men say that when the khamsin blows
for five days straight it can drive a man to kill,
as if such hot murders should be excused.
In Hebrew, the word for "wind," *ruach*, is the same
as the word for "soul." But in Arabic there are more

than fifty different words for "wind," just as
in the Koran alone there are more than one hundred and fifty
different ways of saying
"God."

A Cyclops's Eye

In the morning when the sun is slant, she walks along the Nablus
Road, through the Damascus Gate, toward the place the Jews call
the Temple Mount and the Arabs call Haram esh-Sharif, the Noble
Sanctuary. In the Old City, she strides through the Muslim Quarter along El-Wad, her Nikon swinging against her ribs. Already it
is very hot and the air is ripe with smells of dust and dung. A jet
traces a chalk line across the sky, the far end blown to haze. It is
good to shoot the Old City in this yellow light. The shutter clicks,
clicks: a Cyclops's eye. She shoots buttresses arching across an alleyway, a wooden door braced with rusting iron stays, a grimy-faced
child crouching like a cat, curls of red graffiti along a concrete wall,
an old man in a kaffiyeh setting out tourist wares, a translucent
sickle moon. It is not easy to get past the clichés. She is not far now
from the Wailing Wall, from the crowds of swaying men in black,
davening to the stones. She could go there now—she would have to
cover her bare head and arms, of course, with the blue rectangle of
cloth the guard would hand her at the barricade—and write a prayer
on a shred of paper, press it into a crack between the Herodian
foundation stones. Weeds take root in those spaces, transform-
ing prayers into leaves, into oxygen, into breath. But Susan has no
prayers now. She puts the lens cap back on her camera and turns
away.

Avraham Waits

Avraham waits in the courtyard of the hotel at a table in the thin shade of a palm. He waves the waiter away, checks his watch: the girl is late. He hopes she's had the sense not to go wandering about the Old City alone. He can't imagine why she would have wanted to stay in East Jerusalem; even he's not comfortable here. He fingers a ridge of bristles along his jaw that he must have missed shaving. Lately he's been having an argument in his head with Udi Azrieli, the schlepper who took over the biblical job when he retired. He can see Udi now, sitting across the table from him, fat and smug, his shirt half-untucked, his *kippa* bobby-pinned to a tuft of hair. They've been arguing over a book that's just come out, blowing up the old Zionist myths about '48, arguing that the Palestinians didn't simply flee at the urging of the Arab League but were terrorized by the Jews and driven off their land, that Ben Gurion gave up the best hopes for peace right at the start. What remains when a myth explodes? Avraham should know better than to argue with Udi, but he can't help himself. He says occupation; Udi says liberation. He says apartheid; Udi says return. Udi smirks, picking his ear with a matchstick. He says, We've been waiting for this for two thousand years. Avraham can't remember what he was going to say. The vision vanishes. At this very moment, the real Udi is probably sitting at Avraham's old desk, in his old office on Mount Scopus, looking out at his old beautiful view. Avraham checks his watch again. The girl is more than fifteen minutes late. He's about to get up and call her room when suddenly he looks up and she is there. He hasn't seen her in he doesn't know how many years but there can be no mistaking Leah's daughter. In fact, it could be Leah herself—the way the girl walks, the way she holds her head and narrows her eyes in a kind of squint. And before he can stand she is holding out her hand, American style, and saying, Hey, I'm Susan, and he is clasping her slim fingers in his and he is glad that she is here.

Artifacts

In the flat on Amram Gaon Street, Susan sits at the kitchen table as Avraham chops cucumbers and tomatoes and onions for a salad. Fanta? he asks. It takes a minute before she understands that he's talking about orange soda. No, no, she says, just water please. The knife *thwaks* against the cutting board. She admires the tiny cubes of vegetables he flicks into the bowl. All Israelis seemed to know how to chop at a prodigious rate of speed. Yellow-handled utensils hang from suction cups along the tiled wall above the sink—a sieve, a whisk, a slotted spoon. A woman's touch. Susan only vaguely re-members Avraham's wife, Eva, a small soft woman with a puff of white hair and the swish of a Hungarian accent. The clock on the wall appears to have stopped at 2:17. Perhaps that's what happens, Susan thinks, when you get older: you get stuck in time. Her own closets are filled with artifacts from the past—her old violin in its battered case, a bracelet from an ex-boyfriend, her mother's linen tablecloths. She never uses any of these things, but she can't bear to get rid of them, either. She thinks of her grandmother's gold watch, lost in Kathmandu, with a painful twinge. She remembers reading once about a man who put all of his possessions—furni-ture, CDs, socks, everything—up for auction on eBay. She could see how it would be a relief. Avraham sets out on the dining table the salad, bread, a plate of cheese, and two foil-topped containers of *leben*, and they move into the next room. The flat is less depress-ing than Susan had imagined, and not too hot even on this stifling day. The dislocated feeling she had at the bar the night before is gone. Behind Avraham, on the sideboard, she studies the array of photographs—Eitan's children, Susan guesses, in Purim costumes and swaddling wraps and naked in the bath. She notices another photograph, too, tucked into the edge of the frame of a larger one: a black-and-white of three children posed in the old-fashioned way, a taller boy standing with one hand on the shoulder of a smaller boy, and beside them, propped on a chair, a baby with a bow tied around its hairless head. It comes to Susan that the boys must be her uncles, the baby her mother, Leah. She points, and Avraham says, Yes, it was taken not long after we came to Palestine. Susan stands to look closer and now she can see clearly in the boys' youthful faces her uncles' determined lips and intense round eyes. But the baby, her mother, she does not recognize. It is a baby as boneless and unblinking as any other who holds her in its gaze.

Hazor

Now Avraham has gone to lie down for his midday nap—he has brought the newspaper in with him but it rests folded across his chest, rustling with his breath. No air moves through the open *trissim*. It is hot, hot, hot. In the next room, he can hear the girl moving about—the rasp of a drawer, the screech of a chair—and he thinks how long it's been since he's heard the sounds of another person, a woman, in this house. Then he realizes that what he's hearing is not the girl but the sound of a pickax striking stone and he is standing at the brink of a staircase cut deep into the limestone like the one they uncovered at Hazor, leading to a system of water tunnels underground. Yadin is there, a surgical mask strapped over his mouth against the choking dust—or is it a gas mask?—but then Avraham sees that it isn't dust at all but ash from when the Israelites burned the Canaanite city to the ground in the late Bronze Age. And then Avraham feels himself falling, falling without weight or gravity, and when he comes to a stop he is curled like a dead infant inside a burial jug, tipped sideways underground. He reaches out and his fingertips touch an arrowhead, a bead, a sharp fragment of bone. Then he opens his eyes and once again he is on his bed, the newspaper open on his chest, fluttering softly above his heart.

Revisionist History

Okay listen, Avraham says to Udi, who in his imagination has settled himself on the chaise longue on Avraham's terrace and is cracking his knuckles, one at a time, while the girl bangs around in the kitchen, tidying up. Listen: don't you think we owe it to our children to go back and get the story straight? Don't you think they deserve to know the truth? History schmistory, Udi answers. Just because they call it revisionist you think it has to be the truth? You think you can just go and dig up the truth like some potsherds or Roman coins? Udi's fingers are thick as bratwurst, the nails bitten to the quick. Avraham looks down at his own hands and for a moment does not recognize the mottled skin lumpy with blue veins. But do you understand what happens, Avraham says, when memory fails? Avraham is thinking of the moment he first saw his wife, thirty-seven years ago, in the main reading room of the library at Givat Ram, in that light blue shirtdress with her hair tied back at the neck, even though she always told the story differently, insisting that they met at a party the week before. Even though she's still alive, he can no longer exactly picture her face—her real face, the way it used to be. He tends to superimpose an image from a photograph instead. So is memory a thorn in the sole of your foot? Avraham says out loud. Or is it a lie? Udi laces his fingers together and bends them back. His forehead shines in the heat. Now perhaps you are beginning to understand, he says.

The Impression of Words

The box is still sitting on the table by the telephone. The telephone is black and next to it there is a pad of paper from Bank Hapoalim and three pencils chewed on the ends. On the pad Susan can make out the faint impression of words although the writing itself has been torn off and thrown away. Avraham has taken out a box of photographs, which have been accumulating for more than fifty years, and they are sifting through them, one by one. There are recent color prints mixed with snapshots from the sixties and deckle-edged black-and-whites from earlier than that. Some have dates and names noted on the back, others are of smiling people whose names Avraham cannot recall. They even find a few pictures of Susan and her brothers, which her mother must have sent. Look, Avraham says, handing Susan a snapshot of herself at three in a party dress and patent leather shoes, posing with her mother before a birthday cake. How young her mother seems! In her minidress with long dark hair she looks so young that Susan has to run the numbers twice in her head before accepting that she is nearly ten years older now than her mother was then. Avraham puts the box of photographs away and offers Susan a piece of chocolate. She holds the bittersweet chocolate in her mouth and looks again at the box, which sits waiting by the phone, like a reproach. Zalman left only a handwritten note sealed in an envelope in the top drawer of his desk. Scatter my ashes in Jerusalem. A dead man's words. And what words will there be when the moment comes? No rabbi will chant a valediction, say a prayer. No rabbi will consecrate a heap of crematorium ash. No one will chant the mourner's kaddish, which does not even mention death, but appeals instead for the sanctification of God's name. *Kadosh*: He is holy, holy, holy, beyond anything that can be put in words.

What the Leaving Was Like

Among the things Avraham cannot remember
is what the leaving was like—
how the cases were packed with the good Pesach dishes,
the eiderdown quilts, the Meissen figurine of a boy and his
    mother,
framed photographs, a mantle clock, loose sheets
of piano music, and all those other belongings
that would prove quite useless here in this desert
here in this promised land. He cannot imagine how
the decision was made to leave everything and go,
with two small children and another barely on the way;
how they said good-bye to grandparents, cousins, neighbors,
    friends;
how they walked out of the house and looked back
that one last time, or maybe didn't look back at all,
thinking this leaving would only be a temporary thing.
He cannot remember the journey by sea to Haifa,
if they passed checkpoints or soldiers along the way,
or if it was just like going on a summer vacation—
a train ride, a boat trip, an adventure. It was no Eden
they left behind, but still he feels himself an exile.

He cannot remember a single word of Polish now
except for a lullaby his mother used to sing—
something about a street, a house, a beautiful girl
who once was loved.

What a Scant Residue

What does Susan know about her uncle Zalman?
That he was seventy when he died of a heart attack
in his sleep in the Chicago apartment where he'd lived alone for
    twenty-two years—
That he never went to synagogue and had only disdain for God—
That he kept a subscription to the symphony, where each year he
    sat in the same
center-left orchestra seat to ensure a view of the pianists' hands—
That he had a crooked eyetooth, hairy nostrils and ears,
a fondness for hummus and olives and sweet mint tea—
That he fought and was wounded in the War of Independence
(and so she pictures him then as Ari Ben Canaan in *Exodus*,
romantic and bold, in khaki with a two-day growth of stubble
    rough on his strong chin)—
That he brought her the kind of presents a childless uncle chooses
    for a little girl:
a Chinese necklace in the shape of a fish, a denim purse appli-
    quéd with a heart—
And she thinks what a scant residue a life leaves—
a fistful of facts both random and worn that hardly add up to an
    entire man
the way eyes, a nose, ears, and teeth do not add up to a face.

Nostalgia

In the morning, while the girl sleeps, Avraham stands in the kitchen, watching the pigeons pecking in the gritty light. Already it is hot. He collects a place mat, a cup, a plate, and silverware, lays them out on the dining table for the girl when she wakes up, the way Eva used to do when Eitan came home from the army or university. The box sits on the table by the phone. How different, he wonders, are its contents from the stuff he's sifted through so many times in excavating the destruction layer of a tell, the debris of ancient fire. Often you found the best things there, buried in the ash, the most telling clues: abandoned vessels, cult objects, tablets, seals, bits of carbonized wood and bone. He loved the way it all came together on a dig, the way you had to turn and twist the pieces in your head until they fit. He used to laugh at the volunteers who'd arrive at the site filled with visions of ancient splendor and grow so quickly disappointed when they saw only piles of dirt and rubble, half-dug holes. But where's the city? they'd complain. Look, he'd point out, here's a foundation stone, here's a cistern, here's a retaining wall. But they saw nothing but destruction, a heap of broken stone. *Tęsknota*: the Polish word for "nostalgia" comes to him suddenly, a word he didn't even know he knew, with overtones of sadness and longing the Hebrew did not have. But whatever Avraham might be nostalgic for remains as deeply buried as the rest of his mother tongue he has forgotten or repressed. He considers nostalgia an unnecessary indulgence, like too much chocolate or cigarettes. He pushes his glasses up his nose. Perhaps Zalman was the smart one, to leave it all behind. Perhaps he'd had no regrets, after all.

Life Was Beautiful There

Every Saturday, Zalman went down to the corner to the Nablus
    Café,
where the owner Nabil served him hummus and olives and cups
    of *nana* tea
and sometimes sat with him and smoked a cigarette and talked
    about

whether business was good, when the weather would break,
    whether Sharon or Arafat
was the greater fool. Nabil had a brushy moustache like Stalin's
    and tired, wrinkled eyes.
His eighty-six-year-old mother sat in the back and supervised
    the cook.

Zalman felt at home there, among the smells of cardamom and
    roasted lamb,
the drone of Arabic music, the photographs of old Beirut that
    lined the walls.
He was born in a village in the hills west of Jerusalem, Nabil told
    Zalman once,

a village with stone houses and hardscrabble fields and groves of
    olive trees,
a village that no longer existed. His old mother still had the deed
    to the land,
a slip stamped and lined like a grocery receipt, given to her
    grandfather in 1931,

which she kept in an embroidered purse in her night table
    drawer. She had the key

to her grandfather's house, an iron skeleton key the size of a
    hand,
which hung from a chain looped like a noose around the post of
    her bed.

Nabil cracked the word *key* between his teeth like a sunflower
    seed, blowing
two streams of smoke out his nose. Life was beautiful there, he
    told Zalman,
before '48, before An Naqba—your War of Independence, our
    Catastrophe.

Then they shook hands and clapped each other on the back like
    two old friends
and joked that they were a two-man delegation of peace, shaking
    their heads
over how they'd both come to be in a storefront café in Chicago,
    Illinois.

Susan Imagines

And now he's serving her breakfast, boiling an egg, pouring coffee, setting out half a grapefruit with a serrated spoon, and she sits
with her washed hair dripping onto her shoulders, feeling light
and childlike as if he were her mother trying to get her to eat a good
breakfast before going off to school. Just like the American Colony
Hotel, yes? he jokes. Really, please don't go to all this trouble, she
says, and he says, Nonsense, you must eat. And so she eats, the toast
and jam, the soft-boiled egg, the grapefruit, the coffee, the juice.
He comes and sits opposite her, folds back the morning newspaper,
adjusts his bifocals on his nose. The fingerprints on the lenses glint

in the sunlight, obscuring his eyes. You need to clean your glasses, she says, and he frowns and says, For this dirty news dirty glasses are alright. Then he takes them off and wipes them on his shirt. Now she sees him as he would appear in a photograph she might take, the round lines of his skull and his magnified eyes and his large, expressive hands. How sad, she thinks, to be so alone, but it occurs to her that he could well be thinking the same thing about her, wondering what hidden flaw or twist of fate has kept her unattached as well. And for a moment, she tries to imagine what it would be like simply to stay here, right here in this flat on Amram Gaon Street in Givat Shaul. She could stay in Eitan's old room, sleep in Eitan's old bed. Every night she would sleep the same amnesic sleep she slept last night. Avraham would cook and she would clean the flat and do the wash. In the evenings, they'd sit on the terrace and listen to the sounds of the night. It would be so easy, really, not to go back. She watches Avraham as he reads the paper, and she shakes off the fantasy. Probably he is perfectly happy living here the way he is. Probably she would miss her own life after a short while. Still, she wishes she were the kind of person who could change her life just like that.

On the Front Page

On the front page, another bus bombing.
More than fifty wounded, eighteen dead,
including the bus driver and his child.
The photos show the roof peeled back like skin,
a mangled exoskeleton of steel,
a medic running beside a stretcher,
a flag of plasma hoisted in his hand.

Volunteers with beards and garbage bags
search for shreds of flesh or shards of bone.
Even those who escape dismemberment
will suffer from an endless ringing in their ears.
In Hebron, the photographs show fireworks
and throngs of people rejoicing,
dancing in the streets around a burning car.
The face of the twenty-year-old martyr
bobs on placards above the crowd.
In all this noise you cannot hear
the sound of tears,
only a requiem of rage.

Avraham Decides

It is not until they are already in the car and on their way that Avraham decides this is the place. He pulls the car over at a bend in the
hillside road and for a moment they sit, looking out. There is Har
Nof, he tells the girl, Panorama Hill, and it is beautiful, the view
from here of the Jerusalem forest on this yellow afternoon: there,
across the crease of the wadi, Mount Herzl, terraced with military
graves, and a bit further on, Har Hazikaron and Yad Vashem. To every hilltop in Jerusalem a monument to the dead. There the concrete
apartment blocks of Givat Shaul shine white in the sun, although
from here he cannot make out which one is his. Not far away is the
compound at Deir Yassin—stone buildings, the barbed wire fence,
the heaps of concrete rubble and stone. What's that, over there? the
girl asks, pointing, shielding her eyes from the sun with her hand.
A psychiatric clinic, Avraham responds. A mental hospital. There
is much this girl does not know. Although, in fairness, he thinks,

many Israelis also probably don't remember what happened there, and he wonders whether it is better to have forgotten or, like the Palestinians, to be unable to forget. He opens the car door, steps out into the heat. The girl joins him, and for a moment they stand, looking out at the knobby hills, the eggshell sky. Behind them, the hot engine clicks. The ground is soft with pine needles and chalky yellow-white stones. Yes, here, he says. He knows he should bury the box but he is afraid someone will see them if he takes the time to dig. The girl hands him the box and he holds it to his chest as he slits the seal with his car key. The box is surprisingly heavy. Two or three kilos of pulverized tissue and bone. CREMATED HUMAN REMAINS, the label says. A riddle. What remains? To this riddle, he knows the answer: only the sky and wind and earth and stones. Shouldn't we say something? Susan asks. Avraham looks at the girl, her amber eyes, the uncanny tilt of her head. And then, suddenly, rising all around them, there comes a rustling and a rush like beating wings. The boughs of the pine trees tremble and sway. The wind. It rises at Avraham's back like the exhalation of a long-held breath. The wind has shifted to the north; now the heat will break. Shouldn't we say something? the girl repeats. No, he says. He looks around again to make sure no one is there to see. Then he shakes the box and the dust and ash fly up into the sky.

Eva

From her wheelchair in the geriatric ward of Ezrath Nashim re-served for the most advanced victims of Alzheimer's disease, Eva Bar-On sits with her head tipped forward against her chest, her glasses crooked on her nose, one blue eye askance. Her hands are strapped to the arms of the chair, and there is another strap about her chest. Shalom, Avraham says, and she twists her head and gives him a look as if to say, Who the hell are you? Today is not such a good day. Sometimes she still recognizes him, although usually she does not, and mostly she will speak only in Hungarian, which he does not understand. Our earliest memories are the last to go; they've worn the deepest grooves inside our brains. Avraham bends and straightens Eva's glasses, brushes back her too-short hair with his hand. He has brought some fruit, a tin of jam-filled cakes, which he offers to the girl, who has pulled up a chair and is stroking Eva's crooked hand. Leah, Eva says suddenly, what's she doing here? But as he starts to explain, Susan holds up her hand and says, Shhh. Eva tilts her head and says in Hebrew, *Ma pitom. Metzuyan. Mea achuz.* What's the problem. Outstanding. One hundred percent. *Ken*, Susan says. Yes. Avraham watches the girl's fingers touch his wife's wasted arm the way a different girl, his wife, once in another life, touched him. Eva glares at him out of one cloudy eye. In its center, he can see only the reflection of his own face.

If

In the first light of dawn, the doves call
to their mates, three hollow notes of a descending wail.
The flat white sky peels back to blue.
In her hospital room, Eva Bar-On lies bewildered
by the white sheets, the four white walls, the straps
that hold her in her bed. Outside her window,
in a flowering ash, the doves call coo-coo-coo.
If she could rise from bed and go to the window
she would see the white-flowered tree, the stony hillside,
the scrubby green of the Jerusalem pines,

and across the wadi, the orange sun striking the windows
of the mental hospital at Kfar Shaul, once
an Arab stonecutters' village called Deir Yassin.
The sun flares like fire in the windows of the stone houses.
It flares and fades. Each day the village burns again.
But Eva Bar-On lays no claim to history. She remembers
nothing. Instead she floats in exile from memory,
from herself, furious as wind.
She is there in the darkest dreams
you don't remember: a pressure on your chest,
a flapping of wings,
the faintest tinkling of bells.

I am going to excavate Hazor. I must know about Joshua.
I must know if he really conquered it.

YIGAEL YADIN

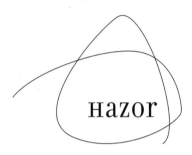

Hazor

Avraham couldn't find it anywhere. He remembered it clearly
enough—a small fabric-bound diary, its pages wrinkled from the
impression of a ballpoint pen, that he'd found in Leah's old room,
nearly forty years ago, as he was clearing out the Sanhedria flat.
But where had it gone? He'd rummaged through the drawers of his
desk, taken down piles of books from the dusty shelves, poked about
in the boxes he kept in the storage space above the bedroom door.
Nowhere. It had been ages, of course—decades, probably—since
he'd seen it last. He wasn't even sure why he would have saved the
thing, this one odd artifact from his sister's youth. He never should
have mentioned it to the girl.

The television was on, turned up loud, and from where he bent
before the open wardrobe, Avraham could hear the gravely tones of
the Tel Aviv archeologist's voice. Over the plaintive melody—reedy
flutes in a minor key—he could make out the words *memory, narrative, mistake*. He straightened with a groan, pushed his glasses up his

nose. The man was photogenic, you had to grant him that, with that dark goatee and curly gray-streaked hair. The camera panned in on the sun rising over the Hebron hills, the rustling olive trees atop the tell, the golden light slanting over the Tomb of the Patriarchs (neatly cropping out the electronic security gate, the phalange of Israeli border guards). *Over time, we have found that the story the Bible tells doesn't exactly fit the facts*. A regular prophet, his distinguished colleague. Knocking down all the golden calves.

What Avraham needed was to get back to work. But the computer sat idle on his desk in Eitan's old room, its screen filmed with dust, untouched since Leah's daughter had come to stay a fortnight ago. Now the girl was gone, though, and he had no excuse. He had to confess he missed her presence in the flat, her company at the dinner table, outside on the terrace in the cooling night. A clever girl. A pity she had not yet found herself a man.

He bent with a groan before the wardrobe and pulled out a drawer, inhaling the scent of cedar and mildew, the odor of decay. Here were decks of cards from the days when he and Eva played bridge. A velveteen case containing a commemorative coin. A glass ashtray swiped from a French hotel. A jar filled with tinny piastres and telephone tokens no longer in use. A discarded eyeglass case, an unwound watch. No diary.

The music from the documentary played on as the credits rolled, an irritating drone. People liked to glorify the past so they could cry that it was gone. He should write an article about that. He shoved the drawer closed with his knee, then picked up the remote and switched the channel to the evening news. Another shooting at a checkpoint in the Gaza strip. The stock market was down. He poured himself a glass of brandy from a bottle on the sideboard, settled into his comfortable chair. He was quite sure he wouldn't have thrown Leah's diary out. But he supposed he would have to write and tell the girl that he was sorry, it just had not turned up.

In the morning, Avraham poured a mug of coffee and forced himself to sit down at his desk. He wiped the dust from the computer's screen with his sleeve, waited for the machine's familiar blink and whirr. Eitan's old bed had been folded back into a couch, the pillows rearranged, as if the girl had never been there at all. He looked out the window onto the flayed trunks of the eucalyptus trees, the kitchen terraces of the neighboring block of flats. The sky had not yet brightened beyond gray. The birds were twittering their waking chorus, hidden in the leaves, their cacophony crowding out Avraham's half-hearted attempts to regain his scholarly train of thought. He pulled his notepad closer, took a sip of coffee, pushed his glasses up his nose.

He missed the university, the fluorescent hum of the institute, his beautiful sweeping view. He couldn't get used to working here at home—couldn't shake the feeling that Eitan might walk in on him, even though his son had grown up and moved away years ago. He always felt as if he were sneaking around the way he had during Eitan's adolescent years, searching for—what? He never found anything, of course, among the textbooks and swimming medals and old toys. Were all parents so baffled by their progeny, all children so opaque? Leave the boy alone, Eva had chided, he's not a puzzle you can solve. Avraham swallowed the last of his coffee, already cold. All people were puzzles. The cursor blinked steadily, expectantly, on the screen. Most of all the people you loved best.

Avraham clicked open his file and skimmed what he had written weeks before, scratching the stubble on the underside of his chin as the argument for maintaining the traditional Iron Age chronology orbited inside his head. How long would he have to go on defending his life's work against the revisionists' claims? He could just see the Tel Aviv archeologist's ironic smile, his eyes unblinking as a hawk's. The truth was Avraham could hardly remember the distinctions he'd made among the thousands of potsherds they'd unearthed, year after year, stratum by stratum, fragments of orange-brown or grayish-yellow clay, incised or burnished, decorated or plain. Pieces of bowls or lamps or storage jars; the bent lip of a juglet, the handle of a pot. The problem was that the evidence could be read so many ways. Any argument was just supposition piled on supposition, a house of sand.

Avraham picked up the book that had been sent to him for review, weighing it in his hands. *The Bible Unearthed*. Already it was a best seller in the States. And what if these revisionists were right? What if Stratum X should be redated from the tenth to the ninth century BCE, to the time of Omri and Ahab rather than of Solomon? What if the United Monarchy—the golden age of King David and King Solomon—was at most a minor tribal chiefdom in the south, glorified for political reasons by the Deuteronomist three hundred years after the fact? What if the Israelites never conquered Canaan, never wandered with Moses in the Sinai wilderness, never came out of slavery in Egypt at all? So what?

Damn the stories, Avraham thought. The evidence was all that mattered. On this point, at least, he and the revisionists agreed. Trying to verify the Bible—he snorted out loud—was a waste of energy as far as he was concerned. He couldn't stand those Texas Christians who came to dig each summer, aglow with earnestness in their search for corroboration of the Bible's text. Or those idiots gallivanting about in search of Noah's Ark on Ararat, or the bones of the pharoah's hordes in the Sea of Reeds. So what if the six-chambered gate and casemate wall dated not to Solomon, but to a later century, a different king?

Avraham pushed back from the desk. It was wrong, that was what.

The birds had given up their singing and the sky had brightened to pale blue beyond the eucalyptus leaves. Already the air vibrated with heat. He was an anachronism, Avraham thought, along with Yadin and Albright and the rest. Only unlike them, he was still alive. He was the one stuck in the wrong century, not the potsherds or the stones. The millennium had passed; archeology was moving on; the revisionists were rewriting history; everything he believed in, had worked so hard for, would be overturned. It was the way of the world. He heard again the music from the documentary, that dismal dirge. It was a dirge for him.

Tell ~ For centuries, it was known as Tell el-Qedah, or Tell Waggas, rising forty meters above the bed of Wadi el-Waggas, fifteen kilometers north of the Sea of Galilee, a two-hundred-acre grassy plateau. A road winds up the slope of the mound, where for a time, there was an Arab village, also called Waggas. You can see it clearly from the air: a bottle-shaped mound lying on its side atop a vast enclosure flanked by massive earthen ramparts and a moat. To the south, along the highway, a swath of bright green bushes marks the springs. To the north, the ridgeline of Mount Hermon hovers like a cloud. Across the surrounding valley stretches the farmland of Rosh Pinah, squares and rectangles of green and brown.

Twenty-two cities lie beneath the bottle-shaped tell, stacked one on top of another like bodies in a mass grave. Dig down through the city walls built and burned and built again by Greeks and Persians, Israelites and Canaanites, invaders from Assyria and Egypt and Babylon, down to the bedrock of the plain first inhabited in the twenty-ninth century BCE.

Then the wind will blow and dirt and grass will cover all your traces, as if you, too, were never there.

Avraham lay in bed, trying not to think about the difficulty of falling asleep, when it came to him with the sudden clarity of a dream that Leah's diary was inside a pigeonhole of the writing desk in the corner of the room. He sat up and swung his feet to the floor, fumbling for his glasses, half-expecting the desk itself to vanish like a mirage. But there it was, potbellied and square, its legs awkward as a giraffe's. He remembered the day he and Eva had found the desk among the clay amphorae and milky Roman glass at the back of a Jaffa shop. Eva had admired its graceful lines, the pattern of vines and leaves carved into the rosewood along the top and sides. Art Deco, the dealer said, from the south of France. A real find. Art Deco my ass, Avraham had whispered in his wife's ear as she started to negotiate. It was almost certainly a fake—he could tell by looking at the grain of the wood and the join how recently it had been made. But no matter—he overpaid; they hauled it home. Neither of them actually used it for writing, of course. Perhaps that was why he'd overlooked it—he'd almost forgotten that you could fold down the lid, pull up a chair. Avraham got out of bed and went over to the desk, turned the skeleton key.

The little book was there. He pulled it out and turned it over in his hands, touching the cloth of its cover, riffling the pages with his thumb. Funny, how objects had a way of turning up like that—it happened on digs, too. He remembered the cuneiform tablet a little boy found on an excavation dump at Hazor, back in the 1960s, as if something had drawn him to the spot, right to the one thing the archeologists had overlooked. The boy had grown up, he'd heard, to become a notorious dealer in fake antiquities. Avraham wasn't especially surprised. He understood that feeling, the incomparable exhilaration of the find.

Avraham climbed back into bed, switched on the reading lamp. It was late now, after one a.m., but he knew he wouldn't fall asleep. He felt the diary's cheap paper between his fingers, examined his sister's handwriting curling across the page. The year didn't appear anywhere in the diary; there was just an occasional notation of the day and month. Leah clearly hadn't written regularly. He guessed that she'd started the diary before she went to the army, before their father died. It was more difficult to tell when the later entries had taken place. The last third or so of the book was blank.

On the inside cover, Leah had copied out the famous poem by Hannah Senesh: *Now—now I'd like to say something / Something more than mere words.* She must have read Senesh's diary in school. Had he even read the diary when he first came across it, all those years ago? None of it seemed familiar now.

He tried to picture Leah, lying on her stomach on her bed, her bare feet kicked up, her arm curled over the page. The windows open to the breeze. The flat ticking in the late afternoon heat. She is chewing on the end of her pen, shaking her hair back from her eyes. She writes slowly, using the words she thinks a real writer would use. *I am caught in the middle of everything, neither here nor there, stuck between my memories and the ever-receding future I so long to reach.* She peers out uneasily from the confines of her bounded universe, a slouchy, self-conscious girl at seventeen, a little overweight ever since her mother died, lively with her friends, silent and insular at home. *It is as if I, as a material body, have simply stopped, suspended in space and time.* It seems as if escape will never come, what she thinks of as her *afterlife*. It is hanging out there, like a prize.

The university was quiet, the students mostly gone for the semester break. Avraham crossed the empty plaza to the institute, stopping by the faculty boxes to pick up his thin stack of mail. He waved to the department secretary, who fortunately was busy chatting on the phone. This would be the first summer in over forty years that he wouldn't be in the field. He was out to pasture instead.

In the office that had once been Avraham's, Udi's light was on, his door open halfway. Avraham poked his head around the doorframe.

Avraham! Udi said, waving him in with a pudgy hand. Sit down, sit down!

Avraham lowered himself onto a chair facing Udi. The desk was piled with stacks of site plans, grant applications, books and journals, excavation reports. Udi's hair had receded even further, if such a thing were possible, in just the few weeks since Avraham had seen him last. Even the young men were ancient here. The place was a goddamned morgue.

Nu! Udi said. How's the life of leisure treating you? He laced his fingers together, pushing them outward with a crack.

Avraham shrugged. He noticed that Udi still bit his nails down to the quick.

So, Udi said, did you catch our good friend Feigelman on television the other night? Son of a bitch never misses an opportunity to create a stir.

What's so bad about a stir? Avraham said. Udi was jealous, that much was clear. Feigelman is smart, he said, rubbing it in. Who's the one with the villa in Herzliya, you or him?

The man just likes to piss on all our founding myths, Udi said, bringing his fist down on the desk and sending a small avalanche of paper cascading to the floor. It's his wife's money, anyway, he added.

I told you he's smart, Avraham said. But he was in no mood to defend Feigelman. The fellow might be smart, but he had his Iron Age chronology dead wrong. Avraham stretched out his legs. So, he said, are you ready for the dig?

Udi ran his hands back over his scalp, adjusted his *kippa*, and leaned back in his chair. It's a disaster, he said. One bus blows up and all the Americans and Europeans hide beneath their beds. We're going in with twenty volunteers instead of a hundred and twenty. Apparently Feigelman's canceling his 2001 expedition altogether! But, as you know, we don't have a choice. The conservation work can't wait.

Avraham shook his head. It wasn't his problem anymore. He would go to Be'er Sheva and visit his grandchildren instead.

Avraham shut the blinds against the light and lay down on top of the sheets, propping a pillow behind his head. From the open windows came the sounds of honking horns, the hiss of a braking bus, the hollow pock of a tennis ball hitting concrete. No one took a siesta anymore, these days. Avraham pushed his newspaper aside, picked up Leah's diary instead. When did it begin? He counted back—she would have been seventeen in 1956—his first season at Hazor. He was just a student volunteer back then, working under Trude in the Canaanite temple and potter's storeroom in Area C. In the expedition photograph taken at the end of that season, Yadin sat in the center of the front row—his legs apart, hands resting on his knees, like the statue of the Canaanite king they'd found among the stelae. Avraham was standing at the back, his shirtsleeves rolled up over his biceps, grinning from ear to ear. Nothing he'd ever done, before or since, came close to the excitement of those times.

Leah would have been at home with Abba then. He pictured her sitting at the kitchen table in the fading evening light, her hair falling forward to screen her face, closed around herself like fruit around a stone. Sounds waft in—the cadence of a Yiddish argument, the crickets' chirping drone, a dog's yowl. *Everyone wants too much from me, but at the same time there is not a single person who really cares.* Why *did I let D. kiss me after the cinema on Saturday night? A huge mistake! Now he keeps sending me such desperate notes—"What about us? Do you ever want to see me again?" I'm sick of these boys. I'm sick of the girls, too, twittering like stupid birds. I'm sick of being a girl, of all the male attention and demands, of having to be nice.* But *nice* is what she is, of course, a dutiful daughter, desperate to please. It is Abba who always wants too much from her, who shouts at her to lose weight, pull back her hair, put on a dress. He has not managed well without a wife. He is an angry patriarch right out of the Bible, punishing and remote. *Who will ever want to marry a lazy girl like you?* As if she should stay home and take care of him instead.

Leah shakes her hair back, stares into space. She is thinking of the way D. held her against the cinema's wall, his tongue flicking against hers, his knee against her groin. His metallic taste, his smell. The way he made her grow so wet. She lives, motherless, in a world of men—father, brothers, teachers, boys from school. Men hold her back, yet without a man, she cannot imagine her escape. *He will be tall, dark, slim, with a strong chin, straight nose, etc.—impossible, clearly.* He could be anyone at all. He does not exist. *I'm sick of* being *a girl*. She'd like to be the one to sail off beyond the Green Line, to Europe or the States, although she doesn't know it yet. She doesn't know that within six years she'll be married in New York, that her father will be dead. She doesn't know how quickly the borders of a life can change.

Cuneiform Tablet ~ The tablet lay on the rubble dump, sunlight shadowing the wedge-shaped marks embedded in the clay. Triangular impressions like headless torsos; horizontal lines like flags stretched out in a stiff wind. One shape like a trident, another like a star. Marks made with a stylus made from a reed cut on a slant. Scratched sideways, from left to right.

They unearthed half a dozen tablets, over the years, though not the royal archive they believed, or hoped, was buried there. They found a record of a fourteenth-century BCE real estate case; a fragment of an Akkadian-Sumerian dictionary; an inventory of goods (textiles, copper, silver, gold) to be sent to Mari, north of Babylon. A list of names and payments: a third of a shekel, or a half. Multiplication tables. A letter delineating a legal dispute.

To Ibni, this tablet began. Was this the ancient king Ibni-Addu mentioned in the Mari archive? Or could it be Jabin, the Canaanite ruler famously overthrown by Joshua? Or an even later king, possessing the same name?

Everything depended on a few lines etched in red-brown clay.

A scratch made by a human hand.

The impression of a wedge.

Avraham skimmed on, noting how the loopy characters of his sister's handwriting became smaller and more regular as time progressed. Was this the way personality consolidated, over time—

growing tighter, more self-contained? He lost track of the chronology, turned back again. *I don't know what to write—there are so many things floating around within me, sticking together in a burning clump, tipping the balance of my moods. I don't know who I am or who I want to be.* She could barely hold herself together, at seventeen. *I feel caught in the middle of everything, neither here nor there.* On the cusp of living, stuck in time.

And what about him? He could not find a single mention of his own name. Yet of course he'd been there all along, there in the Sanhedria flat with her and Abba, except for summers on the dig and those times when he got called to the reserves. But his memory was as unrevealing as the pages of the little book. He must have sat across from her at the dinner table on Shabbat, waited in the hallway for her to finish in the bathroom, rapping at the door. But the only moment he remembered now was one captured in a photograph—not a true memory at all. In the picture, they are standing in front of Abba's brand new car, a Morris imported from England at considerable expense. His arm is loose around her waist. He's looking straight into the camera, his forehead pressed into a frown. *Hurry up.* Leah is wearing denim shorts and sandals; her legs are brown and strong. She is looking off to the side, beyond the range of the lens. They are touching, but not quite.

Somewhere along the way, her handwriting began to change. Somewhere came a marked shift in tone. He leafed back through the pages, checking dates. May. August. May again. When?

She has finished the *bagrut*; she is in the army now, a desk job on the base—that much is clear. She is still living at home, but she's almost out from under: real life has drawn her in. *Well, it has begun! So many new and interesting things are happening, I can hardly write it all down.* She is typing up reports, shuffling paper at a metal desk, answering the phone. She wears a pert beret, a khaki skirt, and a blouse. She twists her hair back into a knot. *It does seem strange that I've only been here such a short while! We are all strangers, from such different backgrounds, and yet held by such a strong, common bond.* Her unit is a mix of the children of old-time socialists, Holocaust survivors, and refugees from Yemen, Egypt, Syria, Iraq, all building the new nation, the fledgling Jewish state. *This "experience" really is important, if only in terms of forcing me to get to know and re-evaluate myself.* But what a provisional thing "experience" is, set inside quotation marks like that. "Experience" is what will happen to her, not something she will do herself. In the end, "experience" can only mean one thing.

And here it is, just a few pages on: *Noticed Y. again this morning, getting on the bus. He is really nice-looking, I think! Dark curly hair, wide dark eyes, straight nose, broad face, long fingers, gorgeous smile. I like him—though I'd better not let anyone find out.* Who is he, this "Y"—a Yochanan or Ya'acov, Yaron or Yonatan? A fellow soldier? An officer, perhaps? *The other day, I thought he had on a wedding ring . . . but today it wasn't there. What kind of situation is that, I wonder?* What kind, indeed. The attentions of an older, married man would be just ambiguous enough to be exciting, illicit but not impossible—such things happened all the time. No one called it harassment, back then.

He could just see Leah in her cap and skirt, sitting at her Under-wood, playing with a loose strand of hair. Stepping up to board the bus, hiking her skirt above her knees as she mounts the stairs. *Then he got on too and sat in front, but after a bit he got up and moved back to where I was!* This is what "experience" was meant to be! She feels her gut contract, the blood rush to her cheeks. *He stayed there next to me the whole ride home! Well, actually, he sat across the aisle, but he was still next to me, except for the open space. I swear he looked right at me a couple of times, and smiled, too. I couldn't speak a word. The whole ride was just one long expanse of time.* This is nothing like the way it was with those high school boys. She is aware that these are the symptoms of a girlish crush, but she wants it to be more. *I think that I'm in love with him! Of all people. Shit.* Her heart beats fast and high inside her throat. His heart is beating, too, right there across the aisle. If a boundary exists between them, it is invisible as air.

The article was not coming along well. Avraham leaned forward, scrolled down to what he'd written the day before. Skipping over the Iron Age chronology, he turned to the question of the Late Bronze Age destruction of Hazor instead. It was written in the Book of Joshua that the Israelites set fire to Hazor in the last stage of their conquest of Canaan. Inscriptions on the Merneptah Stele in Cairo marked the first mention of the name "Israel" in describing the Egyptian victories over Ashkelon and Gezer in 1207 BCE: *Israel is laid waste, his seed is not*—so one could suppose that the Israelites had conquered Canaan sometime in the thirteenth century BCE. But the archeological record was ambiguous at best. While the ceramic evidence dated the destruction broadly to the fourteenth or thirteenth century BCE, it said nothing about *who* set fire to Hazor. The cursor blinked mockingly. He was no Bible scholar or theologian. He'd trusted science, persistence, analytic rigor, methodology. Yet now, after all these years of hard work, he could not confirm a thing.

Avraham knew what the revisionists were arguing. That the destruction of the nearby Canaanite cities of Aphek, Lachish, and Megiddo took place not all at once but over the course of a century or more. That the hill survey evidence convincingly showed that the Israelites were no well-organized tribe, coming out of Egypt to launch a sudden conquest of the land, but a disparate group of nomad-farmers whose identity developed only slowly, over generations, in the highlands of the Galilee.

It made perfect sense. It made no sense at all. If the Israelites didn't destroy Hazor, who did?

The Palestinians were already making political hay out of the controversy, claiming that they, as direct descendants of the Canaanites, trumped the Jews with the more authentic claim to the ancient land.

It was no consolation that nothing could be proved.

Myths created a reality of their own.

Mask ~ He crouched inside a court defined by four low stone walls, part of a Canaanite temple from the Late Bronze Age, just below the ramparts of the tell. He brushed away the reddish dirt, lifted aside a stone. Two hollow eyes. A nose.

He called to Trude—Quickly! Over here! Together they reached down and brushed the rest of the dirt away, touching the long brows and parted lips, the beardless cheeks and chin. The holes for tying string in the center of the forehead, and above and below each ear. From the field telephone, they called Yadin. Come quickly! Come and see!

The face stared up at them like a child at the seashore, buried to the neck in sand. Was it the death mask of a Canaanite child? Or an object associated with a cult? Long after Canaanite times, the Phoenicians depicted the moon god Ba'al Hammon and his consort, a powerful goddess called Tanit. Clay masks found at Carthage—with broad, smooth cheeks and protruding ears, almost identical to this—represented Tanit's face. Was this too a mask of

Tanit? The Deuteronomist called for the destruction of the pagan gods. Did Joshua's men decapitate the statue of Ba'al that this mask would have adorned, set the universe ablaze?

For three thousand years, this goddess face has waited, buried deep beneath the ash. But her blank eyes are blind. Her lips are parted, but she cannot speak.

Avraham sat outside on the terrace, his feet propped on a chair, trying to read in the dim light. It was a windy evening, the air salty, almost sulfurous, blowing in off the Dead Sea. The eucalyptus trees rustled in the dark. There were eucalyptus trees in the garden in Sanhedria, too, shedding their long leaves and curling seedpods over the stony ground. Other trees, as well. There was one low-branched mulberry he used to climb with Zalman, pretending they were in the Palmach, spying on British troops—or trying to catch a glimpse of the fat lady undressing in the house next door. He remembered Leah running to their father to tell on them. He'd decapitated one of her dolls in revenge.

It wasn't surprising, he supposed, that he'd had no idea that Leah was in love—it wasn't as if they'd ever been particularly close. *I've totally lost my appetite; I can hardly eat a thing.* When did her cheeks begin to lose their plumpness, her body to take on a woman's form? It must have been apparent, only not to him. *I was sitting outside, having a coffee with Shlomit, when he walked right by and smiled at me! Shlomit asked me what was wrong, and then she teased that I must be in love. So it must be true! I don't think it was obvious or anything, but I think (hope?) that it adds up. . . . Oh, what am I going to do?!* Even Leah was lost in the calculus of signs.

Avraham ran his finger along the inside seam of the diary, touching ragged bits of paper where a page or pages had been torn out.

Were all diaries written in the consciousness that they might some-day be found? He tilted the book up to the light. *We were eating lunch when suddenly the doorbell rang and my stomach dropped. Abba stopped chewing and asked me if I had a "date"—as if I'd let anyone call on me here! Then Avi came back with a rather bewildered look, carrying a single long-stemmed rose that the florist's boy had delivered to the door. There was a note attached to it, with my name on the envelope, but I couldn't immediately decipher what it said, as it was written in some kind of code.* So he was there after all, holding the telltale rose. Bewildered, indeed. Avraham thought back to his own first dates with Eva, which would have been right around that same time. He certainly never sent her a rose! But he vividly remembered trembling as he waited in the stairwell for her father to answer the door. He had to smile at the thought of his own awkward, youthful self.

Here was "experience," then, breaking over Leah like a wave. *I can't even believe that certain things that are happening are happening and have happened and are going to happen.* But whatever did happen—those *certain things*—were lost now with the torn-out page; only a trace remained. *It all happened so naturally, gently, beautifully, just as I'd imagined that it would. I felt absolutely at ease, not at all guilty or embarrassed, like before. It didn't matter anymore what anybody else thought.* It was still the fifties, Avraham reminded himself. She would have had to sneak out late, after Abba was asleep, through the back gate to the next street. He'd have borrowed a car or army truck, taken her to some out-of-the-way place—a coffeehouse or social club, in the new suburbs to the west. A dim and smoky place with wooden chairs, a Shoshana Damari ballad playing on the pho-nograph. They'd have stepped outside, out of the light, looked up at the stars. *Oh, his curly black hair, his eyes, his hands, his smooth dark skin!* He would have leaned close to light her cigarette, closer to kiss her lips. She feels herself dissolving, growing blurry with desire. *He put his arms around me and lifted me up then and said, Is it really you?* Later, she sits in bed, too overwhelmed to sleep, the diary propped on her knees, her mascara smudged beneath her eyes. *Even as I write this, it becomes more and more unreal, flat and featureless as a slide. Is it really me here? Was it really me there?* The eastern rim of sky is already growing light. Like everything else she longs for, like memory, it shimmers beyond her reach.

Avraham closed the diary, raised himself from his chair, pressing his palms against his lower back. It was very late. All the windows in the neighboring apartment blocks were dark. The stars were out, faint perforations in an orange-tinted sky. The same stars Leah had gazed up at on that different, vanished night.

Did Abba know? He must have, or he wouldn't have packed Leah off to study in the States. Avraham remembered Leah shouting that she wouldn't go, Abba shouting how she didn't know how lucky she was, the envelopes with U.S. stamps stacked beside the phone. He'd never understood why their father had been so adamant, but now, maybe, it made sense. Abba would never have tolerated her carrying on with an older, married man. Avraham picked up the diary and went inside, switching off the terrace light. So Abba knew. Or did he? There was no way to tell. There were no facts, just hypotheses and explanations with relative degrees of plausibility. Who was to say that a diary contained any greater truth than any other artifact? No text could escape the distortions of its own mythology. The truth erased itself as you wrote it down—even Leah knew that. *I have no perspective now—I just wish I could find the words to anchor a corner of this slippery memory that is all I have left.* Avraham turned the key to lock the terrace door, switched off the outside light.

In the kitchen, the Frigidaire shifted gears like a laboring truck. Avraham paused as he passed Eitan's old room, the curve of his desk chair and computer momentarily taking on human form, as if his own ghost were sitting there. Avraham wiped his glasses on his shirt. His eyelids burned—he never should have stayed up so late.

Avraham got into bed but, even as he closed his eyes, Leah's words continued to tumble through his head. *His curly black hair, his eyes, his hands, his smooth dark skin!* Breezy as it had been outside, no air moved through the bedroom windows. It was too hot to sleep. *I think that I'm in love with him! Of all people. Shit.* He turned the pillow over to the cool side, kicked back the sheets. *I'd better not let anyone find out. Oh, what am I going to do?!* What was she so worried about? That he was an officer? A married man? Maybe, but still, something didn't fit. *A single long-stemmed rose.* Sending roses wasn't the style of the officers he knew—not back in those macho pioneering days. The guys he knew just took their girls by the hand and led them straight to bed. (The image came to him of a particular field assistant—what *was* her name, anyway, Shoshana? Shulamith?—who'd come at night to his own kibbutz bed during those first few summers at Hazor.) A single rose, a note in code. Was this Y just a romantic, or did he have something to hide?

He sat up and switched on the lamp again, picked up the diary. The evidence was what mattered. What were the facts? She met him on the bus. He walked by as she was sitting in a coffeehouse downtown. She did not actually say he was an officer. Or a Jew. Avraham had just . . . presumed. *His curly black hair . . . his smooth dark skin.* There were other possibilities as well.

Y stood for Yusuf, too.

It was impossible, but still. Avraham found himself thinking back to the Israeli Arab students he'd had over the years—their politeness, their rather old-fashioned courtly ways, so different from the brash Israeli style. It was impossible, but now that the thought had entered his head, Avraham couldn't get it out again. He could hear the throaty ayins, the rolling rs, as he lifted her off the ground, his eyes locked on hers.

Is it really you?

Of all people. Shit.

By 1959, Leah was in New York. She left the apartment blocks of Sanhedria, the crumbling stone walls and dusty lots littered with curls of rusted wire and weeds, for the steel and glass of Manhattan, the unbounded energy of the States. She stood on the tarmac at Idlewild and felt her lungs expand. She wasn't of the generation who had longed from exile for a mythic land of olive trees and Bedouins roaming with their flocks, for the desert wind, the sound of camel bells. She hadn't realized just how confining Israel was until she got away.

Still, she longed for him. *Last night I dreamed that I was at the beach, singing songs to a guitar. Y. was there and then he began to play and I started to cry. Why am I still thinking so much of him after all this time? I wonder—is he thinking of me, too?* She crosses Washington Square Park in the half-light of a November afternoon, dead leaves swirling before her on the path. She looks up at the brick townhouses with their imposing stoops, the windblown sky. She's fixed up her dorm room with a new bedspread and a potted cyclamen, tacked a travel poster to the wall—*for the first time, I have a room that looks like my own!*—but even so there is something loose inside her, sliding around like broken glass. She clings to the edge of independence, too frightened to look down. *At moments I almost enjoy New York, being here on my own and free. But then there are so many nights like this, when I just feel lonely and self-pitying and sad.* She tries to fill her emptiness with pain, holding Y inside her like an open wound, hating herself for her weakness, welcoming it as evidence that what she felt was real. But already she is having trouble conjuring up the image of his face. It is cracking like old paint.

Soon there's Herb or Richard, Len or Bill, flirting in the college library, taking her out to parties or Greenwich Village clubs. To them, she's an exotic, with that alluring accent and her long dark hair. *Had a fun time being bubbly, losing my voice over all the music and the noise! But I'm afraid I've been too free. . . . Before I knew it he had his arms around me and all I could think was, oh no no no you can't, even though for the first time in forever, I actually felt alive.* These American Jewish boys are nothing like the men back home—with their ties and blazers, their rosy cheeks and slouchy ways, they seem barely formed. They are like newborn rabbits, blinking in the light. What do they know of the world? She lies awake at four a.m., cold and restless, listening to the clicking of the radiator, a distant siren's scream. She has not been back to Israel in more than two long years. In the grainy dark, she tries to picture home. She tries to remember the smell of the kerosene heater in winter, the feeling of the stone floor underneath her feet, the crackly call of a muezzin from a distant minaret. She thinks of her mother, knitting in the rocking chair in the alcove outside her room. If there is another woman there now with Abba, she doesn't want to know. She pulls out her memories of Y, replays them like a tape. She listens for that soft choked sound deep in his throat as he touches her face and whispers, *Is it really you?*

Figurine ~ This time, they would have known the end was near. Word would have traveled of the capture of Damascus, the destruction along the Mediterranean coast, the fall of Ijon, Abel-beth-maacah, Janoah, Kedesh, Gilead, ever closer to Hazor. They broke down their old houses and reused the stone to shore up the defensive walls. They built a tower on the northwestern point, an ashlar bastion with a hidden gate, an enormous storage silo lined with stone. But none of it was any use. The conflagration raged for days, just as it had in the days of King Jabin, five hundred years before. It blackened the foundation stones, left charred beams and plaster strewn across the ground. The ash fell one meter deep and black.

Even now, you will find evidence of the Omrides' decadence and sin, buried in the ash. Here is a woman's ivory cosmetic jar, carved with a cherub and a human figure kneeling beneath a "tree of life." A stone palette with a concave depression in the center for grinding kohl. An incense ladle. A clay figurine of Astarte, the fertility goddess of the cult of Ba'al, her hands raised to her naked breasts. The skeleton of a pig.

The prophet Isaiah shook a finger at the Israelites, now banished from their land. *See what happens when you disregard the ways of God.*

The telephone rang while Avraham was still asleep, penetrating only slowly the fog of a complicated dream. An air raid siren was going off, a burglar alarm, a field telephone. His phone. He fumbled for the receiver, knocking over his clock, squinting in the daylight streaming through the blinds.

Professor Avraham Bar-On?

It took him a few moments to understand that it was a reporter calling, looking for a comment about Feigelman's appearance on TV. The reporter spoke a halting Hebrew with an American accent; when she switched to English, she sounded just like his niece.

Did he believe the Bible contained no historical facts—that the biblical stories were only myths?

It is not a simple topic, he heard himself say, raising himself onto an elbow and trying to clear the roughness from his throat. You can't throw out the entire Bible because some facts don't line up. But you must also understand that with the Bible there is no such thing as objective history, even if some stories contain a core of historical fact.

Would he agree then with the statement that the Patriarchs did not exist?

I don't know, he said. It is certainly possible that they did. But it is also possible that the stories came out of ancient folklore instead. The fact is that the Tomb of the Patriarchs in Hebron wasn't built until Roman times. From an archeological perspective, there's no positive evidence to prove either view.

But couldn't the Palestinians now claim a greater right than the Jewish people to the land?

Avraham coughed. Will anti-Semites make use of these ideas? Sure, yes. But look, here are the facts. At some point the Israelites emerged as a distinct group; about this, there is no dispute. Did it happen in the thirteenth or the tenth or the seventh century BCE? Any way you look at it, we've been here a long, long time. And if we were all Canaanites first, then nobody has a claim over the other at all, right?

So in your view archeology can shed no light on the true narrative of Jewish history, Professor Bar-On?

That isn't what I said.

Thank you very much, Professor, for your time.

The day was a write-off as far as work was concerned. His editor would just have to wait. Avraham put on a baseball cap (a gift from one of the Texan volunteers) and set out for the long walk to Ezrath Nashim. He still felt groggy despite the two cups of strong coffee he'd made after getting that damned reporter off the phone. He walked along the hillside road, ignoring the pain that radiated through his lower back. It was good to walk.

Maybe today his wife would recognize him. He still held out that hope, even though he couldn't remember the last time Eva had had a "good" day. Usually she just muttered at him in Hungarian, or stared into space. Or maybe she'd mistake him for her father, as she sometimes did. The worst days were when she didn't even mistake him for someone else. Who are you? she'd shout, straining at her chair. What are you doing here? It was a good question. Still, she'd been his wife for over forty years.

It was strange, Avraham thought, measuring his pace as the road began to slope uphill, how the biggest events in life weren't necessarily ones you wrote about, the way that you'd expect. Avraham knew that Leah met her husband, Ezra, during those first years in New York, yet he hardly showed up in the diary at all. He was like background noise, a presence but far from the main event, showing up in glimpses between descriptions of trips to Jones Beach with Doris, or dates with Len or Rich or Bill. Ezi was madly in love with her, that much was plain, even between the lines. *I said something about how wonderful it would be to have a child someday, and he gave me one of those* looks *of his and said, "Don't talk like that."* He knows she's flirting with the idea, trying it on like a too-expensive gown.

But he's familiar, a fellow Israeli, a safe bet—a man she can imagine being married to. But is marriage what she wants at twenty-one? *I'm afraid he does care* too *much (and yet I don't want him* not *to care).* She stumbles over the double negatives, trying to convince herself. *Still, he is a good friend and I do feel happy when he's around.* Maybe she's afraid to let him become more than *just a friend.* Or maybe it's more complicated than that. Maybe he simply doesn't make her knees grow weak, her heart rise to her throat. But Ezi is persistent if nothing else. If he can't knock her off her feet, he'll make sure he's there to catch her when she falls.

Avraham stopped in a shady spot near the crest of the hill, taking out his handkerchief to wipe his brow. He was breathing hard, his heart flopping like a fish. Eitan would be angry if he found out he'd walked all this way. He was as imperious as Abba now that he was a doctor; ever since he started to lose his hair, he looked just like him, too. Funny how the genes persist. The breeze riffled through the leaves overhead, cooling the sweat that trickled down his back beneath his shirt. Even now, he could remember the day Abba died as clearly as if it had happened just the other day, instead of thirty-nine years ago in July. He remembered standing in the Post Office, his sweat evaporating in the stale breath of a fan, hollering through the partition to the telegraph clerk. *Abba had a massive heart attack. Stop. Come home next flight Pan Am. Stop.*

But Leah hadn't caught the next flight home. She'd arrived in Jerusalem three days later, after Abba was already in the ground, without even calling to let them know that she was on her way. He almost didn't recognize her when he opened the door and found her there in that short black dress, her hair cut shorter, in a modern flip. He hadn't seen her in over two years. They went together to the cemetery the next day. Leah knelt by the grave and touched the freshly overturned dirt with her fingertips. She picked up a little stone and weighed it in her hand.

Leah stayed in Jerusalem that whole summer of 1962, there in the Sanhedria flat. He and Eva had already moved to Givat Shaul, and for the rest of that summer he was digging down at Tel Arad, trying to make headway on his Ph.D. Leah was hardly a child then, and yet, now that he looked back, he felt guilty for leaving her there alone. He didn't get around to clearing out the flat until after she'd gone back to New York, and he was dismayed to find Abba's toothbrush still on the bathroom sink, his trousers still draped over the arm of the bedroom chair. He had to fight back the urge to douse the place in kerosene and send it up in flames. In the end, he'd packed up the mantle clock, his mother's Pesach dishes and Shabbat candle-sticks, some photographs—Leah's diary, as well. She didn't ask for anything and neither did Zalman. He kept those things, and gave away the rest.

Eva was sitting in a chair to the side of her bed, her head lolling forward, asleep. Her chest rose and fell with each shuddering breath, a trickle of drool pooling in a dark stain on her green hospital-issue shirt. Everything here had a greenish tinge—the walls, the tile floor, fluorescent light on skin. He looked around; there was no other chair. He sat down on the bed instead and, after a moment of consideration, tucked the pillow behind his neck and stretched out his legs. The walk must have tired him out, after all; a spreading fatigue weighed on him like the lead vests used as X-ray shields. They'd strapped Eva to her chair again, and for a moment her arms jerked back against the restraints, then went limp again.

Avraham always talked to Eva, the way people talk to victims of deep comas or catastrophic strokes, as if, at some remote level, language might still get through. He told her about his visit to the university, about the disastrous drop-off in volunteers, the stalled article, about finding Leah's diary. He didn't tell her he had read it, though—she wouldn't have approved of his snooping into Leah's private words. Eva had strict ideas about peoples' boundaries, the limits of one's space. She'd never pried into Avraham's personal things—never peeked into his mail or poked around inside his desk. And because she trusted him, in such a complete and unjustifiable way, he never hid anything from her. Or maybe he'd just understood that she would find out anyway.

A nurse entered with the lunch cart, sliding a tray onto the bedside table, but Eva didn't stir. The nurse frowned at Avraham, muttering in Russian, and backed out of the room. The tray contained a square of grayish meat, some limp green beans and potato cubes, an anemic-looking salad, a cup of chocolate mousse. Avraham stuck his finger into the swirl of whipped cream on top of the mousse and gave it a hopeful lick. But the meal was kosher and the cream wasn't made from milk, and it left a chemical aftertaste on his tongue. He didn't look forward to trying to make Eva eat when she woke up.

Avraham took off his glasses, resting them on his chest, and shut his eyes. Eva would have laughed at his attempts to piece together Leah's story, his fanciful theories based on the most tenuous of facts. Young girls keep secrets, she would have said. The most obvious explanations are usually the truth. Probably she was right. Leah went back to New York, married Ezi, raised a daughter and two sons. She made a good life for herself; no one could ask for more. Still, there was something that bothered him about the last section of her diary, something in the chronology that didn't quite seem right. But right now he was too tired to think. The muffled sounds of the hospital closed over him like water, and he slept.

Burial Jar ~ The jars lay buried in virgin soil beneath the earthen floor of houses built in the sixteenth century BCE. Inside the jars—infants' bones. Tiny skulls and femurs, vertebrae and ribs, curled like crustaceans in their shells. Milk-filled juglets for the afterlife resting by their heads. These were not child sacrifices, as at Hinnom—not with so many burial jars beneath the floor of every house. This was how life was then.

Folded tightly inside wombs of clay, babies dreamed their mothers floating overhead, while underneath the soles of their bare feet, the mothers felt their babies move again as they'd once moved inside of them—the tiny spasm of a hiccup, the ripple of an outstretched hand.

Avraham woke to a sudden scream and shouts.

What is this man doing in my bed? Get him out of here! Out!

The Russian nurse who'd brought the lunch was bending over Eva, trying to stop her from tipping over the chair. It is just your husband, Madame Bar-On, she said. *Spaseeba*, calm down, please.

Avraham sat quickly upright, sending his glasses skittering to the floor. He swung his feet off the bed, squinting to see where the glasses had gone. The room was washed in shadow, and the food on the tray beside him looked congealed. How long had he been asleep?

What are you talking about? Eva shouted, jerking her head from side to side.

Avraham crouched down on his hands and knees, groping for the glasses along the floor. A sudden surge of anger rose like reflux in his chest. Why did he bother? Eva was as good as dead.

Don't worry, the nurse said, bending to pick up the glasses, which had slid beneath Eva's chair. The nurse gave him a thin smile that revealed the glint of a gold front tooth. *She don't know what she say.*

What is he doing here? Eva said again, whimpering now, tears of confusion and rage running down her face.

The glasses were missing one lens, but Avraham put them on anyway and continued to sweep his hands along the gritty floor. There was the lens, over by the bedside table. He snapped it back into place and rose, wiping the lopsided glasses on his shirt.

Don't worry, he said. I'm leaving now.

Out in front of the hospital, a taxi was idling in the sun. Where could he go? Not to the university. Not downtown: since the Sbarro bombing, all the coffeehouses were dead. He fought the urge to get out of the cab and check into the hospital himself. There someone would bring him meals on trays and fresh white sheets. Maybe there he could sleep. The driver twisted his head back, turning up his palms. Nu? he said. Avraham gave up and gave him his address.

He could hear the telephone ringing inside the flat as he fumbled with his keys, but by the time he pushed open the door, it had stopped. With the blinds shut against the sun, the flat had the dim and airless quality of a tomb. It even smelled unfamiliar, after the antiseptic hospital air—it had the stale, decaying breath of an old man. He sat down at the table, leaving the blinds closed. The pile of junk mail, the stained coffee mug, the notepad with its cryptic scrawl, all looked like archaic artifacts, the detritus of someone else's life. He thought of Leah, there in the Sanhedria flat with a dead man's toothbrush and discarded clothes. She wrote almost nothing in the diary that final summer, as if she couldn't bear to listen to her own voice. *Enough drivel about how I feel, enough bor-*

ing self-analysis. Someday I'll go back through all this and think, how could I have thought it was so important? Maybe nothing was worth remembering after all. *I can't write, not today at least. I'm tired of this book, of talking to myself. I never feel that I've quite captured this moment or that scene, having left out, on purpose or by accident, the most important thing. Flipping back now through these pages, all I notice are the gaps.* She'd given up on words, on trying to preserve the past.

She was right, Avraham thought. What was gone was gone. For what was he trying to hang on? He pushed his chair back and stood up, and with sudden resolve went into the kitchen and pulled a garbage bag from the cabinet beneath the sink. Why leave the job to Eitan, after he was dead? He might as well start now. He went into the living room, pulled open the armoire. Into the garbage bag he threw the decks of cards, the empty eyeglass case, the useless coins. His heart was hammering in his chest. The next drawer was filled with archeology magazines and yellowed newspaper clippings, decades old—into the bag they went.

Words, words, words, Leah had written, near the end. *Such a waste.*

So, he thought. Leah went back to New York in the fall of 1962 and got married in October and in the spring of 1963 Susan was born. May, he was quite sure. He counted backward on his fingers. Babies born in May are conceived in August. And in August, Leah was still in Israel; this much was a fact. Had Ezra followed her to Jerusalem? Or had she been seeing someone else? Could it—could it have been Y?

Avraham sank onto the couch and took his glasses off. Here he was, doing it again. Constructing an impossible story from the barest facts. Still, preposterous as it was, it made a certain sense.

He imagined Leah back in New York on Yom Kippur, beating her fist against her chest. She would have known she was pregnant by then. Did Ezi ever consider that the baby might not be his? Possibly Leah wasn't sure herself. Possibly Ezi never questioned why her eyes brimmed so suddenly with the urgent need he took for love, attributing it to her father's death, her lonely summer back in Jerusalem. Or maybe she confessed the truth to him and he used it to secure his power over her, to bind her to him. *We'll get married,* he would have said, *and everything will be okay. No one ever has to know.*

Avraham fetched the diary from his bedside table, flipping quickly to the end. *I hate these layers of memory I carry with me all the time, the tightness in my throat, the tension across my forehead. I try to speak but only hot, weak tears come out; I'm crying even as I write these words. Nothing has turned out the way I thought it would.* Her suffering wasn't necessarily on account of Abba's death. But he would never know.

He went back to the living room for the garbage bag, dragged it to the bedroom and over to the writing desk. He turned the key and pulled down the lid, pulling Eva's things from the pigeonholes and drawers—old letters, notepads, pencil stubs, clippings, matchbooks, photographs. He dumped it all into the bag, continuing until the desk was emptied out. The garbage bag bulged, gaping, on the floor. He walked over to the bed, and after a long moment, threw the diary in. Then he tied the top of the bag into a knot and heaved it over his shoulder, carried it down the stairs and outside to the street. He swung the bag into the green garbage bin, brushed his hands off on his pants. It was done. He would write and say that he was sorry, but the diary could not be found.

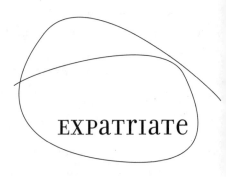

EXPATRIATE

What Leah remembered many years later was that it was May and it was snowing and throughout the city the branches on the budding trees were snapping under the weight of leaves and blossoms and the unexpected snow. She didn't really remember the pain of the contractions or the shaking or the numbness of her legs, other than the fact that these sensations had occurred. She remembered the milky light, the clumps of falling snow. You're nearly there, the nurse had said. She held up a mirror and said, Look!

But Leah didn't look. She turned her face toward the wall. It was only afterward, after they'd placed the baby in her arms, washed and checked, that she drew her breath and looked and saw: skin the color of eggshells, eyes a murky, indeterminate blue. The baby gazed up at Leah, the faintest shadow of perplexity traced between her brows, as if she might have been thinking, Who the hell are you?

Leah felt a loosening in her hips and elbows, wrists and knees, as if she were afloat, a rushing in her ears. She took a breath and looked again: eyes and hair and nose.

You're two peas in a pod, everybody later said. There's nothing in her of Ezi at all!

Back in the early sixties when they were newly married, Leah and Ezi lived in a third-floor walk-up at Columbus and Eighty-first, a cheap rental Ezi had found when he first came to New York. They had bookshelves made from packing crates and planks, a folding bridge table, a phonograph, a couch handed down from a friend who'd gone back to Ramat Gan, a pair of canvas sling chairs (a steal at $7.95 apiece from Klein's), a borrowed mattress on an aluminum frame. None of the dishes matched. But it didn't matter, because soon they would be going back. Once Ezi finished his degree. Once the Frigidaire was paid for. Once they could afford a flat back home.

They were not the only ones; the *hevrei* came together from all over New York. They gathered in dim West Side cafés where you could read the Hebrew papers (only a few weeks old) or play sheshbesh while some newly arrived kid strummed the old familiar songs on a guitar. They gathered in walk-up apartments and basement flats, the air blurring with the smoke of their cigarettes as they argued over coffee and a slice of honey cake about the latest idiocy of the Knesset, or about the spoiled brats Ruthi had to put up with at Hebrew school, or how Cha'im was going to marry his American department store heiress, or how after all this time Yoav had finally made up his mind to go back home.

And they were happy in that way that you are happy when you

are young and everything is temporary and who you are is still a thing that you can try on and take off again as you please, like a new shirt or pair of shoes. They weren't their parents or their grandparents—displaced persons, refugees. They didn't have to choose.

The story Leah always told was that Ezi chased her to Jerusalem the summer that her father died and swept her off her feet. The doorbell rang, she said, and there he was, tall and hairy-legged and resolute, the outline of her future life, backlit by the sun. He saved my life, she said, as if it had not been a decision but a simple matter of her desperation and his desire, her gratitude, his will. He held out his hand, and she grabbed hold.

But in fact it wasn't until weeks later, back in New York, that she slipped beneath the surface and began to sink, bubbles streaming from her nose. She looked up to the surface and saw the light split and refract. She sank as if there were stones in her coat pockets instead of that small white card printed with the telephone number of a doctor she couldn't bring herself to call. Inside her, a living thing swam in the dark. There was a rush and roaring in her ears. Over and over, she counted back. When could it have happened? When?

When she broke the news to Ezi, nine weeks on, the pressure on her heart and lungs so great she scarcely had the breath to speak, he simply sat down at the table in his sleeveless undershirt and took out a piece of paper and a photograph of her. *This is the girl I'm going to marry*, he wrote in ballpoint on the back. He pressed the stamps onto the envelope with his fist. By the time his parents read the letter, they had already been to City Hall. Shmuel and Ruthi popped a bottle of champagne on the steps and cried *mazal tov*. Who needed a rabbi when the sun was shining through a canopy of autumn leaves in Central Park? She wore a short blue dress. She didn't show.

Leah cooked Thanksgiving dinner, that first year of her marriage, for their Israeli friends, their whole *hevrei*. She walked to the A & P on Broadway and bought, on Carol's advice, a turkey (a bird she'd never cooked or tasted in her life), cans of cranberries and creamed corn, sweet potatoes, and acorn squash, lugging it all home in nylon shopping bags that cut into her palms. Carol baked an apple pie. Ezi took the bedroom door off its hinges and laid it across packing crates, covered with a bedspread; they sat, as if it were a seder, on pillows on the floor. They filled their wine glasses and toasted the pilgrims, Ben Gurion, Kennedy, themselves. *L'chaim!* they cheered, for they, too, had survived.

Still, the turkey took far too long to cook, and by the time it was ready, the wine was nearly gone and, even with Carol's tipsy assistance, the potatoes were lumpy and there was no gravy and she'd neglected to warm the bread. She was pulling it from the oven when she heard Ezi's voice ring out. What is this—jam? Leah! What do you think, that we are eating breakfast here?

She stepped out of the kitchen and there was Carol laughing so hard tears were running down her cheeks, trying to explain the concept of cranberry sauce, and Ezi and the others laughing, too, and making faces of disgust. Jam on meat? Ezi was saying, in her father's voice. Meshuga!

Leah ran into the bathroom and locked the door. Ruthi came and tapped and pleaded, and Ezi shouted that it had only been a joke, but like a stubborn child, she would not come out. She sat on the toilet, staring at the black-and-white pattern on the tile floor, blurry through her tears. And then, even though it should have been too early yet, she felt something inside her move—a tiny ripple, like a wave. An ally's secret sign.

Later, Leah couldn't remember her boys, as newborns, ever looking at her the way Suzi did in those first few weeks of life, through irises that slowly turned from murky blue to a strange, amber-flecked brown. She gazed at Leah as if there was a certain knowledge sealed inside her, like a crystal hidden in a geode, sharp and bright. She lost that look with time, of course, as she learned to smile, then to speak. As self-consciousness came trawling like a fisherman's long net across her mind.

Leah held the baby close against her chest and rocked. She sang lullabies in Hebrew and Polish that she hadn't even known she knew. She sang in the half-light of early mornings and darkening late afternoons, as the traffic slowed along Columbus and the shadows lengthened against the walls, trying to picture her own mother rocking, singing, light-years ago. Back in Israel, her sister-in-law had just had a baby too—twin birth announcements for Suzi and Gavi ran side-by-side in the *Jerusalem Post*—but here, she was all alone. If it hadn't been for Ruthi, she didn't know how she would have learned to fold and pin a diaper, to test the temperature of the formula by tapping the nipple against the inside of her wrist.

Ezi, of course, was no use at all. He packed his briefcase and went off every morning to his lab, slept soundly through the night. Still, he touched her, in the quiet hour after dawn, with a tenderness she'd never felt before, holding himself almost unmoving inside her, as he had while she was pregnant, as if the baby might know or wake and hear. She waited for the tensing of his arms, the release of breath against her neck. Only much later did it occur to her that what she took for tenderness might really have been fear. Of her body's elasticity and power, its wild singularity.

People always said that Suzi looked just like Leah, except for the eyes. Who did she get them from? they said. Even Ezi, the geneticist, could not explain. Eye color is a highly complex polygenic system, he'd say, turning up his palms. The molecular basis of the genes is not yet known.

He always spoke that way when people asked about his work, throwing out scientific words like *heterozygous* or *multihybrid* or *allele*. He sketched diagrams full of letters, capitals and lowercase, and went on about Gregor Mendel and his peas.

No one understood the importance of what Mendel discovered, Ezi said, until thirty years after the fact.

This Mendel, Leah said. He was a Jew?

Ezi frowned and lit a cigarette. No, no, he said. He was an Augustinian monk. The famous peas he grew in the garden of his monastery in Brno.

Leah wished she had a garden. Instead, she kept geraniums, begonias, cyclamen, and a spindly palm in pots along the windowsills, shifting them to the fire escape when the weather got warm enough. Maybe she would grow peas, too, someday. Sweet peas, with curling tendrils, twisting vines. Tendrils like a baby's hair.

She placed Suzi on a sheepskin carpet on the floor and went back to pasting photographs into the album she was making for Ezi's parents. She picked up a picture of her holding Suzi, bundled in a hooded towel, in front of the mirror after her bath. Both their mouths were rounded into a perfect *o*. Who's that baby in the mirror? she was saying. It was their little game. Ruthi said four-month-olds couldn't tell. Beneath the photograph, in white ink on the album's black paper page, she wrote in Hebrew, *Mi zeh?* Who's that?

They went to Israel nearly every year. They rented a flat for three weeks in the summer across the street from Ezi's parents, took their meals with them. They sat around with army friends on Shabbat, drinking Nescafé, picking at a bowl of grapes, the babies playing at their feet. They argued over Eshkol and Nasser, the discoveries at Masada and the Dead Sea, the successes of the kibbutzim, whether the lira could ever be shored up.

Their friends in Israel always said, Nu, so when are you coming back? It was not really a question. It was an accusation, a matter of loyalty.

Next year, they always said, and they meant it, at the time. Next year Ezi's fellowship would be up. Next year they would have saved enough to buy a car.

So they went to the beach, took day trips to the Kinneret and Caesaria and Tel Aviv, but after a week or two they began to feel claustrophobic and bored. They shopped for gifts for the secretary in Ezi's department, souvenirs for their American friends: jewelry set with green Eilat stones, embroidered blouses from Maskit, olivewood candlesticks, wall hangings decorated with arches and blue domes. They exclaimed over the quality of the Jaffa oranges, the Tnuva cheese. But at night they lay in their borrowed bed and whispered how expensive everything was here, how Yoav was not satisfied with the equipment in his lab, how Nir was earning barely half of what an ophthalmologist could make back home. *Home.* They turned off the light and lay sleepless in the dark.

Back in New York again, everything felt oversized. Even their own apartment, with its twelve-foot ceilings and bay windows, felt out of scale. They sat around the table on Indian summer afternoons with Yitzhak and Carol, or Shmuel and Ruthi and their kids, the fans blowing grimy air through the windows. They complained about LBJ and Lindsay, the potholed condition of the roads, the declining standards of the schools. They didn't like the idea of their children growing up in such a materialistic society, they said, not to mention all the drugs and crime, hardly noticing that they'd switched to English, unable to find the word they were looking for in the language they spoke less and less frequently but never stopped thinking of as their own. The plank-and-packing-crate shelves had come down long ago, the card table replaced by a Danish Modern dining set in teak with matching chairs. They fanned themselves with sections of the Sunday *Times* and said, It's a khamsin! forgetting that the gritty yellow khamsin wind was nothing like this humid heat at all.

The baby's face was a familiar landscape or a completely foreign land, depending on the light. Leah leaned over the crib in the dark, scanning anxiously for the faint rise and fall of breath beneath her ribs, as if life itself were something so tenuous it could simply be exhaled in sleep. Even as she watched, the baby's forehead, nose, and mouth changed shape, took on an alien form. Her skin wouldn't have had to be any darker, nor her hair any curlier, for her to be someone else's child. Leah understood why there were changelings in fairy tales. She didn't even recognize herself in photographs anymore.

Leah's face had grown more angular in the months since Suzi's birth; she'd let her hair grow out, and was thinner than she'd been in years. She did everything one-handed, the baby balanced on her hip, like an extra limb. She washed and bleached the diapers and strung them on the line; she starched and ironed Ezi's shirts, beat the carpets over the railing of the fire escape, waxed the kitchen floor. Years later, she could hardly believe she'd done it—all those obsolete domestic tasks! And she'd hooked her shopping bags over the handles of the baby carriage, and lugged it—baby, carriage, groceries—up those three steep flights of stairs. Only once in a while, after she'd put the baby down to nap, she'd climb out onto the fire escape to smoke. She'd sit there cross-legged on the slatted steel, tipping her ashes into an old coffee mug, looking out over the chimneys and TV antennae, the rows of brownstones and apartment buildings, to the river running south to the harbor and the open sea, and she'd feel her stomach hollow out and the air rush against her skin, the way she'd once imagined she would feel when she was grown and free. Maybe her own features changed, too, then, just for a moment, out there on the fire escape, her face held to the wind. Maybe, just for a moment, she became that shadow-self she'd left behind in Jerusalem, flush with longing, plump-cheeked and bold.

But then the baby would wake and start to call, *ima-ima-ima*, and Leah would push back her hair and stub out her cigarette in the mug, crawl back into the living room, straighten her blouse and jeans. From the bedroom, her fists gripping the rungs of her crib, Suzi watched and called. She stood there like a stalwart little sentry, sounding the alarm. From the beginning, she guarded the frontier.

Leah dreamed she was climbing a steep staircase, a red-leafed Wandering Jew plant growing out of her head, hung like a Christmas tree with fish and silver charms. She woke with a dry mouth, her heart knocking in her chest. She shook Ezi's arm.

It had snowed overnight, and the early noises of the city rose muffled, as if wrapped in felt, from the street below. Ezi rolled over and pulled her to him in the watery half-light. She wrapped her arms around his waist and tipped her hips toward his. This time, there could be no doubt.

The baby, a girl, was born alive at twenty weeks, but Leah never held her or even saw her face. She weighed barely a pound, the doctors said; her lungs were immature. She drowned, Leah understood, in air.

It is just primitive superstition, Ezi said dismissively, to blame a dream. Biology was biology; such things happened for the best. But what did he, a man, know of those twenty weeks she'd shared her body with another soul? She could feel it still, in quiet moments, floating on the stubborn currents of her lymph and blood.

Only Suzi, who was not yet two and far too young to understand, showed signs of distress. She began to thrash wildly in her sleep, her eyes unnaturally open, rolling in her head. The pediatrician said such night terrors were not uncommon in children of this age and assured Leah it would pass. Ruthi said, Try buying her a doll. And so without asking for an explanation, Leah took Suzi on the cross-town bus to Alexander's and picked out for her a baby doll the size of a real six-month-old with a soft pink body and plastic head and legs and arms. Suzi loved the doll and, as if by magic, the night terrors immediately stopped. And it wasn't long afterward that Leah became pregnant again, first with Jonathan, then Noah. Boys that looked like Ezi, self-contained and tall.

They didn't think of themselves as expats. They weren't like the Americans in Paris or the British in Nairobi or Bombay, who wore their nationality like a badge. They weren't immigrants, either, like the Puerto Ricans and Dominicans who'd taken over the old Jewish tenements in Harlem and the Bronx. An immigrant came for good, and they always knew they would go back. They were fiercely proud of their strappy fledgling country, though there were times when they did not let on that they were Jews. Nearly everyone in New York came from somewhere else—the Midwest or Italy or Iran. Ezi had a German accent, after all; Palestine was not really his fatherland, Hebrew not his mother tongue. Even Leah had spoken Polish first. Israel was their homeland now, of course, but their roots did not grow deep. Maybe they were incapable of growing roots at all.

Or maybe it was the world itself they didn't feel at home in, this swirling blue-green planet that looked so tiny from the moon. They didn't feel at home in their own skins, those loose accretions of half-forgotten languages and disparate cultures' ways. Only the children changed all that, made them feel like something more than particles adrift in space. The children twined around them like ropy strands of DNA, like the ivy that pressed its tendrils into the crumbling mortar of their building's walls. It wasn't true that you gave your children your identity along with your genetic code—it worked the other way around as well. It was because of the children—with their perfect English, their Americanness, which rose off them like the sweet smell of their skin—that they moved to larger apartments, applied for green cards and to private schools, accumulated appliances and furniture and toys. For the children's sake, they stayed.

Just for now, they said, while the children were still small. When they're old enough, they'll go to the army, of course, and meet there a nice Israeli girl or boy.

They played records on the phonograph, Hebrew ballads and the old patriotic songs, ate the canned olives and tahini sent by relatives from Israel along with glossy calendars decorated with photographs of Galilean wildflowers and native trees. They went back to visit in the summers, socialized with their gang of Israeli friends. They spoke Hebrew at home, for a while, but stopped because they worried the children would have trouble when they went to school. They planned (but never took) a sabbatical year in Tel Aviv. What more could you do? Genes split and recombined. The children were American, as indecipherable as an unbroken code.

What if? It was a question Leah never asked much when she was younger, but once she became a mother it took hold of her like a stubborn vine. What if Suzi stopped breathing in her sleep, or fell and hit her head? What if she tipped over in her high chair, leaned too far out the window, got abducted, murdered, lost, mugged, run over by a bus? What if there were race riots in the city, or a nuclear attack? Leah clutched the children's hands in hers as they walked along the street, those moist and pliant little fingers that had once grasped onto her own pinkie so firmly in that reflexive infant grip. Be careful, she warned. Watch out.

What if? The universe was not a fixed continuum of space and time, as she had once supposed, but cut through with possibilities that could open up like a sinkhole on Tenth Avenue. If her parents hadn't run away from Poland when they did, if her mother hadn't died so young, if Ezi hadn't come to her in Jerusalem—what then? She wrapped the familiar contours of her daily life around her like a shawl. She sat on the beach by their rented cottage at the Jersey Shore and watched the children playing on the sand, Suzi and the little boys. The waves were big today, rising up quite suddenly, then curling over and crashing into foam. Noah jumped up and ran into the water, a plastic bucket in his hand. Before him, the next wave reared up. Watch out! Leah called. The wave folded and broke; the children turned and ran, laughing, faster than the water foaming at their feet.

Once, Leah had gone swimming late at night in the Mediterranean near Ashdod. She'd gone there with her troop of scouts; they'd set up camp among some Roman ruins—toppled columns, a broken bit of wall—on a bluff above the sea. She'd climbed down to the beach after dark with two of the boys to sneak a cigarette. It must have been a moonless night; she remembered the sound the waves made rising in the dark, their disembodied crash and hiss. The boys went swimming first, whooping and calling out. She stayed on the beach after they'd pulled their clothes back on and headed back up the bluff. Then she stubbed out her cigarette, undressed. The water closed around her, cool as a mother's hand on fevered skin. It didn't even cross her mind that it might be dangerous to swim. It was a few minutes before the set of waves came in—she barely registered the pull of the undertow, lifting her slightly off her feet, before the first wave broke and hit her, knocking her beneath the exploded surface with such force that she skinned her knees and elbows on the rocky bottom and came up choking, her hair full of sand. Somehow she crawled onto the shore, coughing, saltwater and mucous streaming from her nose. It would have been a while before anybody noticed she had drowned.

Suzi might have looked like Leah, but by temperament she was her father's girl. Like Ezi, she was watchful, resolute. Always asking questions, wanting to know why. At the same time, she gave Leah the impression of a thing closed in on itself, like an oyster around a grain of sand. Even as a little girl, she rarely shouted or threw fits. She bruised in places Leah could sense but couldn't reach; she shied away, all jutting elbows, knees and chin, when Leah tried to fold her in maternal arms. She offered little information about herself, rarely bubbled over with excitement or dissolved with disappointment or bad news. In spite of herself, Leah felt betrayed. How could her own daughter—her likeness, ally, coconspirator from the start—be so different from her?

That's how it is with mothers and daughters, Ezi said, as if that explained it, but he came from a family of boys. Maybe she and Suzi were, in fact, too much alike. It was as if Suzi could see right through her, probing with those strange amber-flecked eyes of hers the places Leah needed most to hide. Suzi had a judgmental quality that must have come straight from Leah's own father—that same tinge of yellow disappointment in her eyes. Leah couldn't blame her, really. She herself had hoped for more.

You must make your own money, have your own career, she told Suzi. Never be dependent on a man. She turned her head away from Susan to exhale, stubbed out her cigarette half-smoked. Tobacco spilled from its split side. She pictured Ezi, standing at the door, his hands stuffed into his pockets, so young and sure in that white light. But then, she'd had no choice.

As time went on, Leah lost the pleasant jolt of recognition she'd felt in the early days when she spotted Israelis on the street. She no longer smiled when she passed them—the women in too-tight leggings and uncomfortable-looking heels, shopping bags looped over their arms, the men with bellies protruding over cheap denim jeans—but looked away, like a child embarrassed by its parents in front of friends.

Have a look at your countrymen, Ezi would say, rolling his eyes. They'd become a principality of two, she and Ezi, an island nation of their own.

Back in Israel, their friends had long ago stopped asking when they were coming back. Those who'd stayed bought houses in the territories, or redid their flats, closing in the terraces and putting in air conditioners and Swedish dishwashers, washing machines, granite countertops.

We have everything here now, they said. Just like in the States.

Their kids wore Nikes and T-shirts from the Gap. Israeli shop-keepers now sometimes mistook Leah for an Anglo, though her own kids still teased her about her English, and Americans often couldn't understand her on the phone.

It's not the same as when we were young, they said. Things are different now. There were cranes hovering across the Haifa skyline, high-rises going up, cell phones ringing, fast food restaurants, checkpoints, supermarkets, shopping malls, Russian street musicians holding out their hats. There was crazy talk, of kids refusing to go to the army, of building a fence to keep the Arabs out, or of giving all the land they'd fought so hard for back. Look at her nephew Gavi, such a sweet child once; what had possessed him to go and join a cult? Where was that old spirit, that sense of purpose? The world had rotated out from under them, but they had stayed the same. How was it that the soldiers hitchhiking at the bus stops were now no more than kids—just look at those girls with miniskirts for uniforms, their caps set at such irreverent angles on their hair! Could these be the daughters of the women whom Leah had grown up with, those robust, fearless sabras who could bake a cake as well as they could shoot a gun?

Leah stood in the souvenir shop next door to where the Super-sol used to be, on the *merkaz*, picking over the plates and vases, knickknacks made from olive wood and colored glass. You could no longer find any good Yemenite embroidery or silver filigree;

even the ceramics were irregular and smudged. You are looking for something special? the shopkeeper said in English. Leah shook her head. She'd been thinking of buying a *finjan* for Suzi, but there were none to be found—everyone preferred espresso machines, apparently, these days. How had everything she loved about Israel become so clichéd, so out-of-date? She was no different from all those tourists staying at their hotel, cameras looped around their necks, accumulating souvenirs. She was a tourist in her own country, like any other Diaspora Jew.

Leah could never get used to the idea that you could just hop on a bus or plane and in a few hours get off again in Amman, Cairo, Luxor, Sharm-el-Sheikh. Even East Jerusalem, part of Israel for over twenty years, still felt out-of-bounds. It was as if the borders she'd grown up with had remained in place, like the invisible fences people put up nowadays for dogs. Despite all the treaties and reconciliations, the old Green Line still held its power to deliver an electric shock.

But Ezi wanted to go to Petra. He brought home travel agency brochures for tours to Jordan, full of photographs of the famous striated formations of colored stone. He propped the brochures on the kitchen table in front of Leah, against the potted cyclamen. Everybody says it is something fantastic, not to be missed, he said.

Leah shook her head. Did he really want to sit on a bus with forty fat tourists with cameras around their necks? Wouldn't it be terribly hot, down there in the desert, south of the Dead Sea? And what was there to see, anyway, besides a bunch of rocks?

Petra. It was a place that, to Leah, had never quite seemed real. Back in the early fifties, when Leah was fourteen, five boys had stolen across the border in search of the Nabateans' two-thousand-year-old city cut into the sandstone. None of them came back. The story made a great sensation at the time—former members of the Palmach, heroes of the war, murdered (everyone presumed) by marauding Arabs, cut down in their prime! The uproar, Leah thought now, was due maybe as much to the tragedy as to the insolence with which the boys had gone and crossed the border—the frontier of civilization as they knew it, the horizon of the imaginable world.

Maybe that was why Ezi wanted to go. Jewish history didn't interest him much—Leah knew he couldn't have cared less whether the walls her brother Avraham dug up dated to good King Solomon or bad King Omri. It was pure romance that he sought in the outsized pillars of the temple of Isis, the ruined amphitheaters and banquet halls, the play of desert light on crimson, rose, and ocher stone. Leah remembered, at fourteen, trying to imagine the five boys sneaking out of Jerusalem on that August night, following the old Roman road to Jericho, crossing the Allenby Bridge, continuing along the abandoned British railway line through Wadi es-Sir, Madaba, Hesbon, Kerak, passing broken tanks, roofless guardhouses, Bedouin encampments, oases, camels, minarets. When they got to Petra, did they climb the canyon track at dawn, looking out over the vast necropolis beneath the white-hot sun, their shirts wrapped like kaffiyehs around their heads? Did they lie at night by the hissing embers of a fire and watch the stars reel through the dark? Did they find what they were looking for? Were they changed?

Leah took a sip of tea, picked up the brochures. The cyclamen was flowering, and Leah fingered its furled pink buds, pleased—it was a cutting from a plant she'd had for years. Those boys from Petra would have been close to Ezi's age, well past middle life by now. But they were long disappeared, like all the boys of that Palmach generation, and here she was, still conjuring oases, camels, minarets, desert light, and mystic stone: all the old romantic clichés. She shifted on her chair and looked out the rain-flecked window at the familiar brown brick expanse of the ugly apartment blocks next door. How long she'd lived here! The place she was from had grown as remote as the stone city in these glossy photographs, and equally unreal. She propped the brochures back against the plant's flat leaves. She'd give them to Suzi when she saw her next. Maybe Suzi would go instead.

BODY COUNT

In the morning she pulled the news stories off the wire. There were always a few familiar bylines; the rest scrolled along her screen anonymous as soldiers, every sentence ranked and measured, every voice the same. Today, again, the news was the West Bank. Israeli tanks were rolling into Hebron, Nablus, Ramallah, Bethlehem, Jenin. Arafat's compound was under siege. Palestinian gunmen were holed up inside the Church of the Nativity in Bethlehem. In the Balata and Jenin refugee camps, there was fighting in the streets. Three Palestinian gunmen, four Israeli soldiers, dead.

Susan glanced across the newsroom as she finished punching the long string of numbers into the phone. There came the sound of what might have been the muffled rumble of thunder, or workmen rolling something heavy on the floor above. In Israel, Debbie's cell phone rang and rang with a whirring tone. Then her recorded voice came on the line, first in heavily American-accented Hebrew, then in English, and Susan hung up. Debbie Nelson was a good reporter, well connected after years of stringing for American newspapers, more valuable than ever in this environment of cutbacks and corporate squeeze. Susan had heard that Debbie had once been married to an Israeli, and even though she wasn't Jewish, she had stayed. Susan had met Debbie a few times on her periodic visits to New York. She was a short woman in her late thirties or early forties, with girlish bangs and doughy, freckled skin. Susan couldn't get over the feeling that she and Debbie should have traded places long ago.

Susan picked up the phone again and tried Debbie's home number, but got voicemail there as well. In Jerusalem it was already late on Friday afternoon, Shabbat. Susan jiggled her mouse to reactivate her screen.

DATE: April 5, 2002. Israeli helicopter gunships launched a heavy attack on a Palestinian village today, killing the man alleged to have planned the Passover Massacre, the suicide bombing that left 26 people dead at a Passover Seder in the Israeli city of Netanya on March 27.

Susan wondered if Debbie had gotten through the checkpoints into the West Bank. She'd have to go with what was on the wires for now.

At six-thirty it was raining, really pouring, the water sheeting off the overhang in front of her building, the roadway rippling with a layer of water pockmarked by the pelting rain. All the cabs seemed to be full or off-duty, sending up sprays of dirty water as they passed. Susan gave up waiting, put up her umbrella, and began to walk toward Ninth. Water dripped off the edge of her umbrella onto her new pointy-toed shoes. She put her head down and picked up the pace.

A group of them always met at Bellevue's on Fridays after work, and its only virtue, as near as Susan could tell, was its proximity to work. Susan pushed open the door, shaking off the dripping umbrella, scanning the crowd for somebody she knew. The place was already packed, kitschy eighties heavy metal blaring from the jukebox. Fake rats and rubber heads hung on grimy walls. Reid was sitting at the bar with his girlfriend, Kristin. Susan didn't recognize anybody else.

She pushed her way to the bar and touched Reid's arm. He was wearing an olive-drab photographer's vest and had a three-day growth of beard. She said, Did you just get back?

Hey, he said, swiveling around on his stool. Kristin gave a little wave. Susan laid her umbrella and bag on the floor, smoothing her hair with a wet hand.

Susan had always found Reid handsome, but there was something—the delicate symmetry of his almost-pretty face, his greenish eyes, his thick wheat hair—that made her feel at times as if you'd have to peel back the skin of his face, like in a bad movie, to find out what he really looked like underneath. It wasn't vanity, Susan thought, that gave him that quality of inaccessibility, but the self-consciousness that came from knowing that, even pasty forty, "good looking" was how he'd always first be read.

There were no free seats at the bar. Susan stood behind Reid and Kristin, feeling her wet nylons sticking to her toes inside her probably ruined shoes. From the back, Kristin looked as wraithlike as ever, her shoulder blades jutting out in two sharp planes beneath the thin fabric of her shirt. She had a mass of frizzy reddish hair and an angular jaw and cheekbones softened by a curvy upper lip. Kristin was getting a Ph.D., writing about something to do with female saints. In some ways, Susan envied her—it would be nice, for once, to write about a subject that wouldn't change, to write without a deadline, to have time to sit and think. Kristin lit a cigarette, blowing the smoke out of the corner of her mouth, in the opposite direction from Susan and Reid. She gave off a tense, airless quality, a sense of disorder held in check.

Yuck, put it out, Reid said, fanning the air.

Kristin raised her eyebrows and looked to Susan, holding out her cigarette at arm's length.

Susan shrugged. It doesn't bother me, she said. Her mother used to exhale the same way, blowing the smoke away from her. Now Kristin's gesture made her feel childish, excluded, and she wished Kristin would offer her a cigarette, even though Reid would give her shit, even though she didn't smoke.

So how was it over there? Susan said to Reid. She'd seen some of the amazing photographs he'd sent back from Afghanistan: veiled women, tribesmen on horseback, American troops in dusty trucks, a landscape of bare brown mountains and cracked-earth plains. As much as she longed to escape New York, it was hard to imagine spending a month in a place as featureless as that.

The bartender set down two martinis in front of them, both an alarming shade of red.

She'll have one of these as well, Reid said.

No, I'll just have a Corona, Susan said, and then to Reid, So how many Al-Qaida and Taliban guys do you think we really got over there? Susan knew that the Americans claimed to have killed over a hundred fighters, but fewer than fifty bodies had actually been found. She looked over at Reid's vest. What could he possibly keep in all those pockets—gum wrappers, condoms, swizzle sticks, wads of Kleenex, lucky stones?

Fucking Shahikot, Reid said. Have you ever been inside a cave?

Yeah, sure, she said, feeling a tightening inside her chest. It was a smugness they all had, those reporters and photographers who'd been there on the ground, bearing witness, bringing back the news.

Shahikot, Tora Bora, Kristin said in a breathy voice that you had to strain over the thumping jukebox to hear. She said, All of those places sound made up to me.

The Afghan names did sound rather like something out of Dr. Seuss, and Susan smiled. She glanced at Kristin's forearms, at the skin so translucent it was nearly blue across her wrists, the ciga- rette tipped between her fingers, and wondered suddenly if Kristin and Reid actually had sex. He was too good-looking for her, Susan thought, and Kristin was too—too self-contained. A small surge of connection rose in Susan's chest. Maybe they'd be friends.

On Monday, Debbie filed a piece saying that the Israelis were pull- ing out of Qalqilya and Tulkarem but that the fighting in Jenin was growing worse. She quoted the director of the Jenin hospital say- ing that Israeli tanks were not allowing ambulances to evacuate the dead and wounded from the camp. *The Palestinian Authority issued a statement today claiming that "the Sabra and Shatila massacres are being repeated in Jenin."* Here in New York, it was still raining. They were predicting that it might change over to sleet later in the day. In Israel, it was probably nice and warm. Once she'd gone with her cousin Gavi to the Galilee to pick irises and anemones in the spring. She cradled the receiver against her shoulder, squinting at the screen.

Can we really say that it's a "massacre"? she said.

We're not saying it, Debbie said after a slight delay, the PA is.

Susan scrolled down the page. *As many as 100 Palestinians have been killed in Jenin alone.* The line crackled, fading in and out. Where are you, in your car? Susan said. You sure about a hundred? We need attribution. Yesterday we said seventy-four, over the past ten days, and not just in Jenin. And what about the Israeli side?

A hundred is what everyone is saying, Debbie said, her voice abruptly clear. And from what I've heard, she added, it's probably much worse than that. But they're still not letting journalists into the camp.

Susan backspaced over *as many as* and typed *at least* instead. She looked at her watch. It was getting late. Okay, she said. I'll see what Bill thinks. If I need anything else, I'll call you back.

Across the newsroom, Bill, the foreign editor, was on his phone. Sipping her coffee, Susan flipped through the pile of clips on her desk, pausing on a photograph of a group of Palestinian militants gazing out from an arcade. They looked curiously relaxed, leaning on their guns, green Hamas bandannas tied around their heads. She'd never been to the West Bank, even though the border was less than twenty miles from her grandparents' Haifa home. She'd driven through the Arab villages in the dry hills east of Haifa, her parents pointing out how primitive they were: the women in their long robes and headscarves; the men sitting outside broken-down coffeehouses smoking hookahs or playing shesh-besh; the cinderblock houses with roofs of corrugated tin, the dirt yards with chickens pecking in the dust. They wouldn't even have electricity if it weren't for us, Susan's father always said. Most of the refugees in Jenin had fled those same villages. Fifty-four years ago, next week.

She tried to picture the foothills of the Carmel, the mountains of the Galilee, greened by the spring rains. She remembered the excitement of arriving in Israel for summer visits as a child, bouncing on the edge of the backseat of her uncle's car as they drove from the airport in Lod up the coast to Haifa, sounding out the Hebrew signs. They always arrived at dusk, the humid air already weighted with dew, the evening sky a luminous pale blue above the shadowed streets, like in that painting by Magritte, *Empire of Light*. And it did seem surreal, the memory of the crunching gravel along the path to her grandparents' flat, the echoing of the doorbell, the silhouette of her grandmother appearing in the light, her powdery and perfumed smell, her frail embrace.

And what if she'd married an Israeli, like Debbie had, and had gone to live in Israel? She might have found herself one of those strong and tough Israeli men, like Paul Newman in *Exodus*, or Yoni Netanyahu, martyr of the Entebbe rescue raid. Or a Mossad agent with secret scars and a sabra's vulnerable core. She might even have joined the Mossad herself, learned to pass on information, to encrypt messages in code.

Bill was standing in front of her desk, looking down at her over his bifocals. He held out his hand.

Deadline, he said.

Kristin met Susan at her apartment and then they walked to a nearby West Side diner for lunch. The manager showed them to a booth in back, across from two young mothers with their babies and a prodigious array of sippy cups and bibs and gear spread out over the table. Susan slid awkwardly into her side of the booth, stashing her jacket and bag next to her on the vinyl seat, and unfolded the oversized menu. She'd often eaten alone at a diner much like this back when she first started work. She always sat at the counter and had salad with cottage cheese and half of a canned peach. She worried about her weight back then, even though she'd always been quite thin. Never as thin as Kristin, though; she wasn't as much of a fanatic as that.

The waitress came and Susan asked for a Greek salad and a Diet Coke, and then regretted her restraint when Kristin ordered a cheeseburger and fries; apparently, Kristin was just naturally that thin. The mothers at the next table were sharing a piece of pie, picking at it from opposite sides of the plate, their heads bent together in conversation. The baby nearest Susan was hurling Cheerios onto the floor.

So how's the writing coming along? Susan said.

Kristin sighed the way Ph.D. candidates always seemed to do when you asked about their dissertations. She was researching the female mystics, she said, slowly, as if trying to choose words that Susan could understand. She was looking at the way patriarchal culture laid claim to the interpretation of their bodies, fetishizing them, labeling them as witches or hysterics or saints. As she spoke, Kristin's voice lost its breathy quality and she leaned forward across the table. She was rereading the women's own writings against the hagiographies and scholarly accounts. Are you familiar with any of them? she said.

Susan shook her head. Jews don't do saints, she said.

They punished their bodies in all kinds of incredible ways, Kristin said, leaning forward. Mary Magdalene de Pazzi made her fellow nuns bind her to a post and whip her; then she dripped hot wax into her wounds. Angela of Foligno drank water containing a leper's putrid flesh. Saint Rose slept on a bed of broken glass, stone, potsherds, and thorns. Catherine of Siena wound iron chains so tightly around her waist they became embedded in her skin. She flagellated herself, licked pus from a beggar's cancerous sores.

She literally ate almost nothing, and eventually starved herself to death.

The waitress set their food before them on the table. Susan looked at her salad, the gleaming olives and clumps of feta cheese. Are you serious? she said. Why?

Kristin said, Some scholars argue that self-mortification, or abjection, is a way of claiming one's own identity, of affirming the borders of the self, in essence, by defiling them. Kristin bit into her cheeseburger, licked a smear of ketchup and meat juice off her lips, and raised her eyebrows. It was also, she said, a pretty good way out of getting married and having kids.

In ninth grade, Susan had been friendly with an anorexic girl. At lunch, Terry fiddled with her lettuce, or broke up a single cookie into pieces on her plate. Her hair grew limp, her skin sallow, stretched taut as a corpse's across the bones of her face. She never walked but ran everywhere, a frightening, feeble shuffle, her heavy book bag clutched between her arms. In the locker room mirror, even though Terry turned away as she undressed, Susan could see the jutting ribs and spine, spindly femurs, and jutting pelvis of a concentration camp survivor. Terry left school halfway through the year for the hospital, where the rumor was she was force-fed through a tube. Susan never saw her again after that. She recalled the plush beige carpet in Terry's bedroom, the white lacquered princess bed, and wondered what Terry was doing now. She hadn't thought of her in years. She'd never considered the possibility that Terry might have starved herself to death.

At the next table, the mothers were picking up squeaky toys and plastic cups, buckling their babies into strollers. The mother nearest them bumped into Kristin as she pulled on her coat, and Kristin rolled her eyes.

Kristin probably wasn't even thirty yet, Susan thought. Why did guys go out with women who were so much younger than they? She wasn't sure, now, what she'd thought they would have in common, after all.

By Thursday, the ninth day of fighting, reports were coming in that the last gunmen had surrendered in Jenin. Debbie had left a message saying that rumors were flying that the Israelis might finally let journalists and aid workers into the camp and that she was heading to the West Bank. Susan pulled the wire stories and a few quotes from an interview with Prime Minister Sharon on Fox TV and set to work on an early edition draft. Maybe this would be the end. She flipped through her pile of clips. On Tuesday, thirteen Israeli soldiers were ambushed and killed by a ten-year-old suicide bomber in Jenin. Yesterday, eight were killed and twenty-two wounded on an Egged bus east of Haifa by another suicide bomber from Jenin. Just this morning, six were killed and seventy injured by a female suicide bomber at a crowded market in central Jerusalem. Susan knew that market well. She wrapped her arm around her stomach and pushed her hair back from her forehead. Palestinian civilians, women, and children, were dying, too. How much worse it had to be for them: she had to remember that. Five hundred dead, they were saying now, maybe many more. She turned back to her computer screen.

According to the Palestinian Authority, hundreds of civilians were killed in Jenin. The PA has formally asked the United Nations to investigate reports that soldiers massacred civilians and buried them in mass graves. How could we have done that? she thought, then caught herself. *We.*

She clicked through the latest photographs: a Palestinian boy walking along a deserted alleyway, a Red Crescent ambulance parked by a barbed wire barricade, a Merkava tank against a backdrop of twisted rebar and shattered concrete, a D-9 Caterpillar bulldozer before a smashed-in wall. Looking at these images, it was impossible not to think of those other bulldozers digging day and night in that apocalyptic rubble pit here in New York. Just last month, they'd pulled two more bodies from the debris. Susan didn't know which felt more real, the images in her memory or the ones before her on the screen, or those that were missing altogether, those of the three suicide attacks. Even though she didn't envy Debbie the ratty, scrappy, poorly paid job of a freelancer, she felt more than ever that she should be there instead of Debbie, who was probably driving north now into the Galilee, passing the dusty villages, the green scrub of tomato fields, the yellow ripple of wheat. Or maybe she was already through the checkpoints, waved on by those IDF boys with their laced-up boots and M16s and youthful Jewish faces beneath their helmets; or already in the city of Jenin, breathing that mix of diesel fumes and dung and dust and garbage rotting in the sun, in that jumble of two- and three-story cinderblock apartment houses clustered along the slope of the ravine. Was she stepping over the bodies of Palestinians in the narrow alleys of the camp? Would she find the traces of mass graves?

The words vibrated on the screen, seraphs and numerals and quotation marks rattling like bones: *occupation, apartheid, slaughter, resistance, terrorism, genocide.* Behind those words it was impossible to perceive the facts. *Militants have pledged that they will turn Jenin into a "Palestinian Masada."* How slippery the metaphors. *What we are seeing here is a terrible human tragedy, a Holocaust against the Palestinians.* How easily the Israelis were cast as Nazis, the Palestinians as martyred Jews.

She looked up and noticed Reid standing across the newsroom, outside the photo editor's office, leaning against the wall. He was sipping coffee from a blue-and-white paper cup and chatting up one of the girl reporters from the City Desk. Once, years ago, just after they'd first met, Reid had asked Susan out. She was still living with her ex-boyfriend then, but Reid had tried to talk her into it anyway. How could she could be seriously involved with someone who wasn't Jewish? he'd asked, and she remembered how annoyed she'd been by his presumption, and even more annoyed by her guilty sense that he was right. It hadn't occurred to her until then that Reid was Jewish; his looks certainly gave nothing away—the straight lines of his nose and jaw, his blondish hair. And now he was the one going out with an expert on Christian saints! They'd missed their chance, she and Reid, back then.

She must have been staring, because just then Reid looked up. And for a moment it seemed as if he was trying to tell her something as he held his gaze on her, but didn't smile.

A group of reporters was already clustered on the ratty couches at Bellevue's on Friday evening when Susan arrived. A few of them moved over to make room for her as she shouted her hellos over the Poison song pounding on the jukebox, whose speakers were uncomfortably close to where they sat. She craned her neck; Reid and Kristin weren't there tonight. Next to her, a young reporter named Derek was swirling the ice around in his glass, and Susan remembered that she'd once read that advertisers subtly hid images of naked female bodies in the photographs of ice cubes in liquor ads to make the drink subliminally appeal to men. She squinted at Derek's glass, and thought maybe she did detect a sensuous curve. Or maybe you just saw what you were looking for.

Next to him, Rajiv was saying, It's always like, hey you with the brown skin, you must be a terrorist. I have to get to the airport at least three hours early now.

Well, at least they're checking, Derek said. I'd be more concerned if they didn't check.

A City Desk editor with thinning hair and round horn-rimmed glasses leaned forward from the adjacent couch. You've been getting some nice front page play this week, Susan, he said. Good stuff.

Rajiv was waving his hands. You know, they're always like, so where are you from? And I'm like, uh, New Jersey? Duh? He made a face and tipped his beer bottle to his lips.

Yeah, thanks, Susan said to the City Desk guy, whose name, she finally recalled, was Frank. But you know how it goes. Mostly I just cobble together other peoples' stuff.

Frank shook his head and frowned. I just can't see how it's going to end, he said. When one side has an army and the other side has nothing at all.

Just suicide bombers, Susan thought, but didn't say. Like the "heroic martyr" who'd blown herself up in Jerusalem today. Palestinian leaders had gone on TV to applaud her act, calling for more. Surely the deliberate murder of civilians was different from self-defense? Surely it was no excuse to say they had no other choice? But there was no point in arguing with Frank. There was something about him that Susan thought of as typically American, a starchy sort of moral earnestness that irritated her, even though there was nothing unreasonable in what he'd said.

Is anybody hungry? Frank said, glancing around, his eyes resting on Susan. Feel like going to get a bite to eat?

He really wasn't unattractive, Susan thought, and it wasn't as if she had any other plans. But inside she felt tight, wound around herself like a spring. For some reason, the image came to her of Terry, back in high school, breaking that single cookie into pieces on her plate. The self-denial of the saint.

Thanks, she said, shaking her head. But I really should be getting home.

Over the next few days, the list of accusations grew. On TV, reporters stood in front of dramatic backdrops of razed buildings and burned-out cars, describing the atrocities that allegedly had taken place inside the Jenin camp. The Arab news networks were now claiming that four hundred, or eight hundred, or twenty-eight hundred, or three thousand Palestinians had died over the past ten days; that thousands more had been arrested and detained; that the Israelis had opened fire on ambulances and paramedics and used Palestinian civilians as human shields; that they'd executed disarmed fighters and left women and children to die as armored bulldozers razed their homes. The Israelis, for their part, were saying that the entire camp was booby-trapped, that the terrorists had mined their own houses, planted detonation charges in the roads, placed snipers inside minarets and schools, commandeered Red Crescent ambulances to transport terrorists and arms. They'd found photo albums filled with pictures of children with notations indicating when each one would be ready to carry out a suicide attack. AP quoted a woman who claimed to have seen at least ten people killed before her eyes and said she came across dead bodies every two to three meters as she fled the camp. Reuters quoted a man who said he'd watched dozens of corpses being carried off in military trucks before dawn. Others reported the stench of rotting bodies coming from rubble overturned by refugees searching for missing relatives and friends. None of the reports could be refuted or confirmed.

But did *you* see any bodies? Susan asked Debbie, pressing her fingers into her free ear. They were jackhammering on Thirty-third Street, a broken water main, loud even here in the windowless newsroom on the eleventh floor.

I didn't, no, Debbie said.

Susan shifted the phone to her other ear. What about the smell?

Look, Debbie said, we were in an IDF armored personnel carrier the whole time. I couldn't smell shit. But let me tell you something: the whole place stinks. The water and electricity have been cut off for days; the garbage is piled up a story high. The camp looks like it's been bombed. Entire fronts of buildings sheared off by bulldozers. The center of Hawashin has been bulldozed completely flat. If there were bodies under there, you'd never know.

Susan hung up and reread Debbie's piece. *Israeli officials put the Palestinian death toll at less than 100, but the director of Jenin's main hospital said the number killed could reach as high as 400 once all the bodies had been uncovered.* She stared at the vibrating words until her screensaver flashed on, a photograph of her brother Noah's kids. His two-year-old was wearing a T-shirt that said "Lock up your daughters!" in colorful bold type.

They were all implicated, Susan thought, in this tangle of images and metaphors, deliberate and inadvertent lies. She knew that Bill would cut the bit about ambulances being used to transport munitions (unsubstantiated) and add a disclaimer about how none of the claims could be verified (true). International human rights organizations were being called in to investigate. But it didn't matter. Already it was too late.

After filing, Susan took the subway home and went out for a run. The early evening sunlight was soft and clear, a strong wind rippling the flags along Central Park West. She crossed into the park, running slowly at first, picking up the pace as her breathing settled into a steady beat, following her regular route to the reservoir track. The high-rises of the Upper East Side hovered beyond the new green leaves, glinting orange in the setting sun. Her lungs expanded behind her ribs; her abdomen pulled taut against the waistband of her shorts. It was good to feel her body: muscles, ligaments, blood, and breath. Her body seemed to grow lighter as she ran, as if her bones were aerating, losing mass.

On the way home, she sprinted the last few blocks, her legs whirring with fatigue, raising her arms as she slowed like a racer breaking through a finish line tape. At her building, she bent forward, her hands on her knees, trying to catch her breath. When she raised her head, he was standing right in front of her. For an instant, she didn't recognize him.

Hey, Reid said.

Susan wiped her forehead with her forearm, still panting. Are you here to see me? she said. She wouldn't have thought Reid even knew where she lived.

Reid shrugged. I was in the neighborhood, he said. Thought I'd see if you were in.

Well, come on up, I guess, she said, pulling open the door.

In the apartment, Reid looked around her living room, studying the spines of her books along the shelves, admiring the view over the Hudson, and then settled himself on the couch. Susan leaned back against the window with a glass of water, conscious of how flushed and shiny her face must be, of the outline of her nipples through her nylon running shirt, of how the crotch of her shorts was damp with sweat. She shook out her ponytail, smoothing her hair back with her hand.

Hey, check this out, Reid said, reaching into his bag. He handed her a portfolio of photographs, large format, black-and-white. I just found out two of them are going to be in a show next month at the ICP, he said.

That's cool, congratulations, Susan said.

The photographs were from Rwanda. There were no close-ups of children or soldiers at checkpoints, no hazy panoramas of refugee camp tents: just bodies. In some of the photographs, she couldn't even tell at first that they were bodies, but realized, on inspection, that what seemed at first to be abstract patterns of darkness and light were in fact enormous heaps of machete-hacked limbs. The bodies were twisted and bloated, piled nine or ten deep, Tutsis or Hutus, staring, white-eyed, identical in death.

That was back in what, 1994, right? Susan said.

Nearly a million Tutsis and moderate Hutus were massacred in one hundred days, Reid said. Boggles the mind, doesn't it, numbers as large as that?

I can't get my mind around any numbers these days, Susan said. But she was thinking that a million you could call a massacre. You could call that an atrocity.

Reid leaned forward and cleared his throat. You know, I was

thinking, he said. Maybe we could hang out together one of these days.

Susan looked up from the photographs, the words reverberating in her head. Reid was giving her a hard, expectant look. She noticed that the skin along Reid's jaw was irritated where he'd shaved. Clean-shaven, in a button-down shirt, sitting there on her white couch, he looked completely different, she thought—boyish, even vulnerable. Or maybe it was just a matter of context, or scale. She crossed her arms over her chest. What was that youthful euphemism he'd used? *Hang out.*

So what's up with Kristin? she said.

Reid shifted on the couch. It's pretty much over, he said.

Pretty much? Susan said.

She waited, feeling his gaze against her skin. What did he see? He hardly knew her, really, at all. Across the living room, through the open bedroom door, she could see the edge of her unmade bed, a tangle of sheets. She pressed her arms harder against her stomach, but already she was unraveling, twisting on a thread. Bodies came together, bodies came apart—what difference did it make, really, in the end?

Reid stood up then and stepped forward, pulling her to him so close she could feel the quiver of his eyes on hers, the exhalation of his breath. She opened her mouth to speak, but he shook his head.

What are you so worried about? he said.

By the end of April 2002, Israel was still blocking a United Nations fact-finding mission from investigating the charges of a massacre in Jenin, and Palestinians were still saying Israeli soldiers murdered thousands of civilians during the eight-day operation in the camp. The Israelis called the claims a blood libel and said they'd found only forty-three bodies in the rubble; the Jenin Hospital confirmed that fifty-two camp residents had died, but continued to hold out the possibility that more corpses might be unearthed. Arafat's compound in Ramallah was still under siege. Palestinian gunmen were still holding off Israeli troops inside Bethlehem's Church of the Nativity.

Same old story, isn't it? Bill said. We'll run six inches on page nine.

Susan shrugged. There would be no untangling the mess. Her e-mail box was full of messages saying that they'd been overly eager to report a dramatic massacre that hadn't really taken place. Even where the words were evenhanded, one particularly irate letter said, the photographs reinforced the anti-Semitic image of the Israelis as brutal bullies, the Palestinians as innocent victims. Had she been taken in?

She picked up a copy of the paper and turned to the photo essay they'd run the previous Sunday, scanning the now-familiar images of toppled buildings, burned-out carcasses of cars, walls sheared off by bulldozers or punched through by trucks, women in headscarves picking through mountains of rubble bristling with twisted metal, shreds of clothing, a propane tank, a satellite dish, a headless doll. In one photograph, a group of little boys sat on top of a heap of debris beneath a red, white, and green–striped Palestinian flag, draped over them like a tent. They were shirtless, their bodies brown and lean. There were plastic buckets at their feet; perhaps they were searching for their families' belongings, or for scraps of copper or aluminum to sell. One of them, she noticed, held what appeared to be the muzzle of a machine gun between his legs. He couldn't have been more than nine or ten. He gazed, gap-toothed, straight out of the photograph at her, as if he had something urgent to say.

On Saturday, the buzzer rang before Susan was even out of bed. Squinting in the sunlight, she shuffled barefoot across the living room to the door. The intercom crackled. It's Kristin, the voice said.

By the time Susan had pulled on a pair of jeans and run her fingers through her hair, there was a knock at the door. Kristin stood there, her hair loosely twisted in a frizzy knot, her skin blotchy and pale.

Well, come in, Susan said. Let me put some coffee on. You kind of woke me up.

Kristin walked over to the window and stood there, her back to Susan, looking out. Through the kitchen pass-through, Susan could see the sharp planes of Kristin's shoulder blades, the shadow of her spine. She felt a twist of apprehension; involuntarily, she braced herself for flying things: an ashtray, a glossy magazine, a book.

Kristin crossed into the kitchen, and Susan handed her a mug. Did something happen? Susan said. Is everything okay?

Kristin's mouth twisted. How could you? she said.

Susan poured milk into her coffee and looked up. How could I what?

He told me, Kristin said. He said he was breaking up with me because he wanted to start seeing you. He told me you'd agreed.

And do you believe that? Susan said.

Kristin set her untouched coffee onto the counter and put her hands over her face. After a moment, Susan stepped forward and put her arms around her. Pressed against her body, Kristin felt even thinner than Susan expected, small-boned as a bird. How strange, Susan thought, to be a man, and embrace such slender, insubstantial things.

Kristin pulled back, wiping her eyes. She shook her head. I don't know what to believe, she said.

I swear, Susan said, we're not involved. It was perfectly, completely true.

By early May, Amnesty International and Human Rights Watch released reports stating that there was no evidence to support claims of massacre or deliberate slaughter of Palestinians by Israeli soldiers in Jenin. The UN put the final Palestinian body count at fifty-four dead, although disagreement remained over whether the bodies were civilians or militants. Twenty-three Israeli soldiers had been killed, not counting the victims of the suicide attacks. But the final numbers didn't matter, Susan thought. The story of the Battle of Jenin would remain a tale of Palestinian martyrdom, no matter what anybody said. And she was as responsible as anyone for that.

Susan logged onto her computer, sipping her coffee and picking at a cinnamon sugar–encrusted muffin in a paper bag. Along with a fresh flood of critical e-mail, there was a message from Debbie with a link to a blurry video clip filmed by an IDF drone of a group of Palestinians carrying out a funeral procession in Jenin. The "body" stood up off the ground after being dropped off the blanket in which it had been rolled and walked away at the end. *Now they're saying it was just children playing a game,* Debbie wrote, *but do those look like kids?*

She called Debbie at home. *Hallo, mi zeh?* Debbie said, just like an Israeli would.

We can't run the fake funeral piece without some corroborating facts, Susan said. Too much crap's gone down already as it is.

Well, it's your call, Debbie said.

There was a rustling in the background, as if Debbie was running water, or opening the fridge. Susan tried to picture Debbie at home in her flat, but this time she drew a blank. She felt it pull at her, the old yearning, across the static line. What are you doing? she said.

Doing? Debbie said. Like right now? Well, if you really want to know, I'm feeding the cat, and then I'm going to drop off Orly at her father's place. It's his weekend to take the kid.

Susan pressed the phone against her ear, feeling it open out before her like a geological rift, this life unfolding in a Jerusalem apartment with cold tile floors and windows open to dry Judean hills, a life with a cat and an ex-husband and a child. Could she see herself there, doing these things? No, she couldn't imagine it at all.

Susan took a sip of lukewarm coffee. In Israel, it was already Friday night. Have a good weekend, then, she said.

Susan hung up, then jiggled her mouse and clicked on the media player to replay the Jenin video clip. She made the blurry "body" fall off and then fly backward up onto the blanket a couple of times, until she tired of the game. Then she clicked the window shut and turned away.

THE PALE OF SETTLEMENT

Her mother told her bedtime stories. The stories were about her mother's childhood and they were always sad. Her mother would sit on the edge of the bed and smooth her hand along the quilt. Once upon a time, she would begin, as if the stories might be made-up tales, the girl someone other than herself.

Tell the one about your grandfather, Susan said. Tell how he was a horse thief and got sent to Siberia. The furrow between her mother's eyes grew deep. He was a Jew from a village near Lwów. Someone told a story that he stole a horse. It makes no difference if it was true or not. They sent him to the gulag anyway.

The places her mother talked about had vanished into a pink blotch that spread across the top of the map that pulled down over the blackboard in Susan's classroom like a window shade. Vilna, Lwów, Bessarabia, Belarus. The Pale of Settlement. You couldn't go to those parts of the world any longer. They were gone.

My grandfather came to live with us after the war, her mother said. Of all the relatives my parents left behind in Poland when they ran away, only he survived. He told stories in Yiddish and held me on his knee. We were each other's only friend. Her mother sighed, a sharp exhalation, as if a weight were pressing on her chest. He died when I was eight.

There was one photograph of Susan's great-grandfather, a passport square distorted by the embossment of an official stamp. His face was gray and grizzled, with hollow cheeks and sunken eyes. His jaw thrust forward, his mouth pressed into a line. Susan imagined him just freed from the work camps, standing like a character in a Cervantes tale beside his loyal stolen horse.

Susan's mother stood, straightened out her shirt. They said his wife never forgave him. For what? Susan said. For abandoning them the way he did, when he was sent away. But it wasn't his fault! Susan's mother pulled up the quilt and tucked it in. Well, no. Now go to sleep.

Susan remembers the touch of her mother's cheek, her accent, her powdery perfumed smell.

Layla tov, she'd say. Good night.

Here is what I see, James said. They were in bed together and it was late. Back in the early nineties, when he was still living in New York but wasn't married yet, James slept on a futon on the floor, overhung with netting like a Bedouin's tent. The walls were painted terra-cotta red, the windows bare and open to the sky. Telling stories was his idea. You had to close your eyes and describe the first thing that came into your head.

He lay back and folded his arms behind his neck. I see a sailboat floating on the sea, he said. A sleek racing boat with polished wood, shiny trim. Only the sails are slack. The sailboat is you. You're bobbing on the ocean swell, waiting for the wind to catch your sails.

What a line, Susan thinks now. Only becalmed was exactly how she'd felt.

She ran her hand along his arm, wrapped her fingers around his wrist. He was a big man and her thumb and middle finger didn't reach all the way around. The back of his hands and arms shone with reddish hair, like a golden idol. Because of this, or maybe because he spoke with an Australian accent, she endowed him with the power of prophesy.

She remembers the orange glow of the night sky, the rumpled sheets, the haze of netting overhead. Your turn, he said. She closed her eyes but what she saw was only darkness, pulsating like space.

Tell me a story, Susan said. Her mother's stories gave her a hollow feeling behind her ribs, as if there was a trapdoor inside her that dropped open to her mother's pain. But she asked to hear them anyway. The stories kept her mother there with her, put off going to sleep.

When I was a little girl, I never got so many stories at bedtime, her mother said. She scrunched her lips together, fixed her gaze beyond the darkened window frame. My own mother was always busy. Always tired. Although sometimes I remember she would sit in an alcove outside my bedroom and crochet. I liked to be able to see her from where I lay in bed.

There were photographs of Susan's maternal grandmother,

doomed and gone long before Susan was even born. She had high cheekbones, pale gray eyes. Cossack blood, her mother said. It was many years before Susan understood that *Cossack blood* meant that someone had been raped.

Susan's mother drew in her breath and let it out, a heavy sigh. My mother married a man from the old world, do you understand? She did not have an easy time. A wife was expected to behave a certain way. My father demanded that she wait on him. She had to have his breakfast ready the moment he was dressed. We had to listen for the shower turning off, the creak of the bedroom door. If she didn't time his eggs exactly right, he would explode. He tormented her, belittled her with words. She was an educated woman, not from the shtetl like him. She was a lovely person, everybody said. But in our house she was no better than a slave.

Susan's mother stood up, smoothed the sheets, tucked them in. Now go to sleep, she said. It's late. Susan took a breath, dug her nails into her palm. But what was it like? When she died? In the doorway, her mother stopped and turned. Honey, she said, I don't think that's something you need to know. Backlit by the hallway light, her features disappeared.

But Susan did need to know, the way she covered her eyes during the scary parts of movies but peeked between her fingers anyway. She heard her mother shift her weight. There was a smell of sickness in the flat, she said at last. Something you'll never know—a terrible smell of camphor. They kept all the windows closed. At night I could hear her crying out in pain. Later, I saw the scratch marks in the plaster from her nails. I shut myself away inside my room and read. Romantic novels. Mysteries. Anything I could find. What could I do? I was just thirteen. No one explained anything to me. One day a neighbor woman came to my room and told me she was dead. She took me by the hand. As we passed my mother's room, I saw that the bed was empty. They had already taken her away.

Now Susan reads so she can fall asleep. She folds two pillows behind her head, props her book against her knees. The bed is broad and billowy with down. Steam rises in the radiators, swirls up from the subway grates on the street below. The alarm clock ticks.

In the novel she is reading: Tel Aviv in the first fall rain. Wet leaves littering the pavement, a low-slung sky, the scudding sea. She's been to Israel many times, but never in the fall. In the story, a young woman flirts with her boyfriend's father. The father is an accountant who can't sleep. The boyfriend, whose mother has recently died, is off trekking in Tibet. The young woman sleeps with his best friend instead. The narrator shows up in his own story, gives his characters advice. Everyone is sad.

Out her bedroom window, Susan can see into the top-floor apartment of a brownstone two blocks away. Every once in a while, late at night, the man who lives there will open the blinds and shine a floodlight on himself. She can't see well so far away, but his movements are clear enough. He unbuttons his shirt, steps out of his pants, takes his penis in his hand. He casts an elongated shadow against the wall. Sometimes she forgets that if her lights are on, he can see her, too.

It's not long before he hunches forward, hurries from the room. She squints, makes out a bookcase, an armchair, a potted palm or fern. An orange poster on the wall. She wonders if she would recognize the exhibitionist if she passed him on the street. It's not unlikely that they've brushed shoulders many times. Then the light across the way snaps off and everything is dark.

It was James's stories that seduced her, the way he made her feel as though he could see beyond the limits of the tangible, straight into her heart. That first night, when he brought her back to his apartment and undressed her and made her come but wouldn't yet have sex, he told her about the Aborigines. They were sitting next to each other on the couch, still behaving as if talking were something other than a precursor to making love.

There was a time, James said, before the world was fully awake, when the ancestors emerged from their underground sleep and began to sing their way across the land. They crossed the continent with song lines, inscribing stories on the landscape, on the rocks and creek beds, rainforests and hills. *Alcheringa*, he said, with his long flat vowels and intense gaze that made her believe everything he said. *Dreamtime*. It still exists, he said, just below the surface of consciousness. He picked up a coffee table book of Aboriginal art, flipped through the pages, reading out the names. Emu Woman. Dreaming Wallaby Man. Susan pictured the ancestors, vaporous as djinns, their bodies cracking through the earth. James pointed to a picture of a hide traced with constellations of tiny dots, red and green and blue and gray. This is the Lizard Ancestor, he said. See, there's his tail. The story goes like this: Once upon a time, the Fringed Lizard and his beautiful young wife walked all the way from northern Australia to the Southern Sea. There a southerner stole the wife and sent him home with a substitute instead.

Susan didn't know then that the book was, in fact, Nicole's. Nicole who imported Aboriginal art for a SoHo gallery. Nicole whose naked body was right there, in black and white, in the photograph hanging on James's bathroom wall.

In those days, James spoke in the singular: *I, my, mine*. Because he didn't talk about Nicole, she didn't yet exist.

We lived in the quarter of Sanhedria when I was a little girl, Susan's mother said. It wasn't a religious neighborhood back then. Behind the house was a garden with some olive trees. My brothers used to climb the trees, pretend that they were spies. All you could really see, though, was into the bedroom window of the house next door. If you were lucky, you might catch a glimpse of the fat Hungarian lady who lived there taking off her clothes.

Susan tried to imagine this part of Jerusalem where she had never been. There were no photographs of her mother's childhood home, so she had to make it up. The bald hilltops, cracked concrete, chalky stones. Dusty plots littered with bits of scrap iron and curls of rusty wire. The wail of a muezzin in a minaret. The smells of cooking cabbage, garbage, diesel fumes. Quilts flapping over terrace rails. The piercing desert light.

The roof of our building was flat, her mother said, painted white against the heat. From there you could see the yeshiva at the corner, the tin-roofed *makolet* where we bought our milk and bread, the old Arab house across the street. The house was made of stone, with a red-tiled roof and windows covered with iron grilles. The family who lived there ran away to Egypt in '48. Al-Rashidi—that was their name. They had a daughter around my age. After they left, the house stood empty for many years. Sometimes my brothers said you could see a strange flickering in the windows, late at night, as if someone were moving around upstairs. Later, they put an army barracks there.

Her mother reached forward, pulled her close. Susan pressed

her face against the softness of her breasts. *Layla tov*. The shadows deepened in the corners of the room. Passing traffic cast rectangles of light along the wall.

Once, years later, Susan asked her mother if what she'd said about the old Arab house across the street was true. What did I say? her mother said, wiping her hands on a dishtowel. How it was haunted, Susan said. How you sometimes saw a light. Her mother made a face, pushed back her hair. Don't be ridiculous, she said. I never said anything of the kind.

Once Susan invited James to her parents' place in Riverdale for dinner on a Friday night. It was still the early days when they weren't really sleeping together yet. She was excited to show him the place she came from, a part of the city he'd never been to before, a place you couldn't get to easily by subway or on foot. She drove and he sat beside her, slightly hunched in the front seat of the Honda, eager as a boy. She took a detour along the Hudson, stopping at Wave Hill. They parked and walked across the sloping lawn and flowerbeds to look out across the river at the view—the flaring red and orange of the autumn leaves along the Palisades; to the south, the George Washington Bridge, strung with lights. A wedding was going on inside the mansion. The bride stepped out onto the stone terrace, surrounded by her bridesmaids, their hair and dresses fluttering like birds. Toscanini lived here, Susan told James, during the war. The wind riffled the hair back from his forehead. In the sharp light, with his wind-reddened cheeks and faint spray of freckles across his skin, he reminded her of her cousin Gavi. A Scotch-Irish version, with reddish hair instead of black, blue eyes instead of brown. God I love this place, James said, shielding his eyes from the setting sun with one hand.

But bringing James to meet her parents had been a mistake. How alien he'd looked, standing there in the doorway with its brass mezuzah, the print of Chagall's green lovers floating on the facing wall. She could feel her parents taking in his ruddy solidity, his height. James O'Reilly? her father repeated as he shook his hand, and Susan felt ashamed. He might as well have had a crucifix around his neck. They followed her parents into the living room and sat stiffly on the couch as if they were foreign guests. You know I spent a month in Israel, James told her parents, when I was seventeen, on an exchange program organized by the Australian government. *Ani medaber k'tzat ivrit*, he said proudly, in an accent that made Susan cringe, but her father exclaimed *yoffi!* and her mother touched his shoulder and said she'd teach him more Hebrew any time he liked. It's a deal, James said as if he meant it, unaware of how they condescended to him, an Israel-loving goy. Susan remembered looking down at the familiar pattern of the Persian carpet distorted by the coffee table glass, trying to decide if her parents thought James was her boyfriend. (They were being so very friendly; surely not.) She remembers noticing James's shoes, flimsy leather slip-ons no American guy would dream of putting on.

After dinner, her parents accompanied them down to the street. They stood with their arms folded across their chests against the wind and kissed Susan on both cheeks and shook James's hand. *Layla tov*, they said. *Az yalla*. Bye. And then Susan and James were back in the Honda, driving south along the Harlem River Drive, back in Manhattan, heading home. She felt, as she always did, a guilty sense of relief at her escape. She glanced over at James, at the line of his forehead and jaw silhouetted in the glare of the oncoming lights, and suddenly it was her parents, not he, who seemed foreign and awkward and out of place. You're lucky, he said. Your parents are great. She remembers the way he reached out across the gear-shift then and took her hand.

The suicide bombing in Haifa on October 4, 2003, is the first to strike a place Susan actually knows well. The Maxim restaurant is down by the beach, adjacent to a Delek station—not a fancy place, but with good falafel and a nice view of the sea. She's been there many times. It's a popular spot, owned jointly by an Arab and a Jew.

The bomber is a twenty-nine-year-old woman, an unmarried lawyer from Jenin. She walks up to the security guard in the glass-walled foyer of the restaurant and detonates her explosive belt. Twenty-one people are killed, including four Arab workers, three children, and a baby girl. Two families lose five members each.

Susan rushes to call her relatives in Haifa when she hears the news to make sure they're all okay. She has to repeat her name three times over the static of the cell phone before her aunt understands who it is. Ah Suzi, she says. She shifts to English. Thank God, everybody's fine. Only the son of upstairs neighbors, a boy Susan and her cousins used to play with when they were young, was there at the restaurant with his wife and kids. They were thrown out of the windows by the blast, but, thank God, survived. If the parents had been there, too, as they'd planned, before the mother got a migraine and decided to stay home, they would surely have been sitting at one of the larger tables near the front. Then they'd all be dead.

After every terrorist attack, cell phones begin to ring. On the charred and bloody ground, in the bags and pockets of the dead, they ring and ring, bleeps and jingles and bits of broken song.

My brother Avi and I didn't get along so well when we were young, her mother said. Turn over, I'll rub your back. Susan rolled onto her stomach, pulled up her pajama top, waited for the touch of her mother's fingers, the reassuring pressure of her palms. My parents favored him and Zalman, her mother said, because they were the boys.

Avraham was an uncle Susan did not know very well. She pictured him as a stolid child with curly hair and hands clenched into fists. She didn't have much to go on, so she superimposed the image of her own brother Jonathan instead.

Her mother ran her nails along Susan's skin, sending a tingle along her spine. Go on, Susan said. Her mother sighed. He ripped up my precious paper dolls. But what did my parents do? Nothing. What did you leave them lying about for? they yelled. Now you'll learn to put your things away.

The curly-haired boy tears the doll, severing head from limbs. He throws the crumpled paper to the floor, stamps it beneath the tire-tread sandals on his feet. He stands defiant, legs apart, fists against his waist.

Her mother withdrew her hand, pulled the covers up over Susan's back. Okay Suzi, now it's late, it's time to sleep. Again that heavy sigh. That weight upon her chest. My brothers didn't have it so easy either, her mother said. My father beat them with a belt, the old-fashioned way. My mother cried, but like everything she did, it had no effect.

The boy's bare bottom is lifted over his father's knee. His pants are puddled at his ankles, his shirt pulled up to expose a sharp white ridge of spine. Thwack! The boy cries out. The father's jaw is set. In the shadows, the mother presses her fingers to her mouth.

It was their mutual friend Patrick who said, You know James really has a thing for you. James? she said. Me? That euphemism: *a thing*—as if something that could not be named could not be completely real. It said something, she thinks now, that Patrick had to say it out loud before she knew. Were there signs she hadn't seen? She knew James from parties, various press events; he was on the business side of the Murdoch empire, a rising star. It wasn't true that she hadn't noticed his eagerness, the way he locked his eyes on hers. He was all forward motion, like a laser beam. She'd just assumed he wasn't aimed at her.

But not long after her exchange with Patrick, James called. Even though she was going out with someone else, she let him take her out for dinner and back to his Hell's Kitchen penthouse. She let him tell her stories about the Aborigines. She waited on the couch, flipping through the glossy pages of the book, while he went and ran a bath. He lit candles along the edges of the sink and dimmed the lights. She let him undress her like a child, lead her by the hand. The bathtub wasn't really big enough for two. He leaned forward in the water, wrapped his legs around her waist, and pulled her close. You are very powerful, he whispered, his lips against her ear. It was an odd thing to say—she didn't think of herself as powerful at all. He leaned back and slid slowly down until his head was underwater, his bent knees lifted high. Bubbles streamed from his mouth and nose. When he sat up, he hit his forehead on the spout, and drops of blood rolled down his face like tears.

It was only later that she took a close look at the photograph hanging on the bathroom wall. There was Nicole, naked as a virgin, lying on her back on windblown sand. Her eyes closed as if she were asleep, or dead. Her hair fanned out along the ridges of the dunes, sea grass arched across her legs. Her skin almost translucent, pale as sun-bleached bone.

Everything looks different in the snow. The city feels muffled, as if it were holding its breath. Susan's own breath condenses before her face. In the park, the paths and rocks and branches are shades of white and gray, the light luminous and blue. It is days like this that remind Susan that Manhattan is an island, a space carved out by rivers opening to the sea. Her boots squeak along the snow-packed path. Her bag, slung like a messenger's over one shoulder and across her chest, swings against her hip with every stride. There are no runners out today. Along the borders of the park, cars are completely buried beneath the banks thrown up by the plows. Funny how on days like these, she feels most at home. Usually she has the feeling that she could live anywhere in the world, even though New York is the place she's always been. When she first started working as a reporter, she'd assumed that she would be living somewhere else by now, a foreign correspondent in some exotic place. She'd be willing to move yet, she thinks, if she only had a reason—even to a place as far away as Australia, though she has only the vaguest idea of what it is like. Dusty ranches and crocodile-wrestling men and strange animals like wombats or bandicoots. And probably not too many Jews, although there did seem to be Jews in the most unlikely places, like Utah or Shanghai.

The Sheep Meadow is a billowy sea of snow. She'd walked with James along this very path, one drizzly afternoon in fall, not long after they first met. Wet leaves littered the pavement; the low-slung sky was gray with scudding clouds. He told her about his father, whom he hadn't seen in years. His father was always making money on some harebrained scheme and losing it all. He'd show up without warning, and then abandon them again. The last time he turned up, James said, he wanted me to invest in some real estate venture up in the north. This one's for real, his father said. James loaned him five thousand dollars, which, of course, he never saw again. He told Susan the story without a trace of anger or resentment in his voice. That's the way he is, he said. He can make you believe that anything he says is true.

Later, Susan made a comment about how his childhood had been tough. Tough? James said. What gave you that idea?

My father, Susan's mother said, was a terrible man.

This isn't the same story Susan has heard from other relatives. They talked about how he saved his family from the Holocaust. How as a physician, he was adored.

He was abusive, Susan's mother said, to everyone except his patients, who worshipped him as if he were a god. He lacerated us with words.

Her mother showed her photographs, flipping through the pages of her grandmother's album. Its black pages were interleaved with translucent onionskin stamped in a pattern of a spider's web. It contained photographs of Susan's grandfather from his medical school days in Germany, in the twenties, leaning like a dandy against a tree, one leg crossed before the other, a cigarette tipped between the fingers of one hand. He had wedge-shaped eyebrows, narrow eyes, a square forehead and jaw. A few of the photographs had holes cut in them: an absence like a silhouette, a body marked by empty space.

My mother did that, I think, Susan's mother said. It must have been the girlfriend he had before he married her.

So she must have loved him, Susan thinks now. In the beginning anyway. Enough to sit there with a scissors in her hand and cut the woman she had replaced out of every photograph. Enough to change the story, excise memory. Susan pictures sewing scissors, the kind with a silver swan's head wrapped around the finger holes. Or was jealousy different than love?

My father kept a row of glass jars in his surgery, Susan's mother said, filled with colored pills. They were sugar pills, although, of course, the patients didn't know that. Placebos. In those days, of course, there wasn't much you could do for people's pain. He measured the pills out carefully, placed them into folded newspaper cones. People took them and were cured.

But how, if they didn't really work? Susan asked.

Her mother's mouth twisted into a smile. Does it matter? People believed they did.

A few months after the Maxim restaurant attack, another woman blows herself up. This time it's a twenty-two-year-old mother of a three-year-old boy and baby girl. She tells the guards at the Gaza checkpoint that the metal detector went off because of an implant from surgery to repair her broken leg. As they approach, she sets off her bomb.

Susan scrolls through clips from the videotape released after the blast. The woman is wearing combat fatigues and a headscarf, a green Hamas sash draped like a beauty pageant banner across her chest. *I wanted to be a* shahid *from the time I was thirteen*, she is saying on the tape. *It was always my wish to turn my body into deadly shrapnel against the Zionists, to knock on the doors of heaven with their skulls.* The rhetoric throws Susan off. Is this a tale the woman was forced to tell, or what she actually believed? Susan studies an image of a crowd of men thronging the streets of Gaza City, their fists raised in the air. It looks almost like an outdoor concert, until you notice the green headbands covered in Arabic script, the placards with the blown-up photograph of the martyr's face. A mother carries a toddler dressed as a suicide bomber, a fake explosive belt strapped around his waist, a toy Kalashnikov clutched in his pudgy hand.

The Koran, Susan knows, says that when you become a *shahid*, you go to paradise, where seventy-two sloe-eyed virgins in long white gowns await. A popular music video on Palestine TV shows a young man joining his virgins after being shot in the back by Israeli troops. The maidens dance in flowing water. They are nearly translucent, white and pure. They wear their black hair long and loose. According to a recent poll, more than a quarter of the children in Gaza aspire to *shahada*, to die for the jihad. Even the girls. Susan wonders what the appeal of the seventy-two virgins would be for a little girl. She should write a story about that. Maybe, she thinks, if all you have to look forward to is becoming a Muslim wife, an afterlife among the virgins wouldn't seem so bad.

James believed in soul mates and telepathy, psychic emanations and powerful flows of energy that you couldn't rationally understand. He used words like *intention* and *bliss*. They sounded odd coming from such a big man, plumped and filled with promise by his Australian vowels. Susan didn't generally put much stock in New Age philosophies, but with James she found herself going along, trying to convince herself that the things he said were true. She lay back and closed her eyes as he recited aphorisms from Rumi, platitudes by Richard Bach. He kept a paperback copy of the *Tao Te Ching* in his briefcase, among the pads of graph paper and manila files. *The tao that can be told*, he read aloud, *is not the eternal Tao.* Coming from him, even the flakiest things seemed wise.

Eventually, he told her about Nicole. He'd met her on a flight from New York to Sydney; at the last minute, he switched seats and wound up sitting next to her. He didn't believe in coincidence; there was no such thing as a lucky stroke of chance. You choose what happens to you in life, he said, knowingly or not. Nicole had dazzled him by telling him things he didn't even know about himself that turned out to be true. Like the Aboriginal women who knew how to tap the power of the Dreaming Track, she had the uncanny ability to read the language of desire. Our souls go back a long, long way together, James explained. We need each other, though we can't stand being with each other half the time.

So what about me? Susan wanted to say. What about me?

But like Scheherezade, she was just a visitor to his Bedouin's tent. She knew he meant it when he said he'd soon be going back to Oz. She gathered up her clothes and left in the flat gray light of dawn.

Her mother sat on the edge of her bed. Tell me a story, Susan said. It's late, her mother said. You need to get your sleep. Susan touched the veins that ran blue as map lines along the back of her mother's hands. Strips of yellow light moved along the bedroom walls. Just a short one, Susan said. Tell about the time when you got sick.

Her mother let out a breath and pushed back her hair. When I was five years old, she said, I got an ear infection. This was before penicillin, the wonder drug. They had to operate to scrape the infection off the mastoid bone. I remember the awful smell of ether, the salty taste of the huge red sulfa pills they ground up in a spoon. They said I nearly died. I was in the hospital for seven weeks. My parents left me there alone. My father—the doctor—was busy working, and my mother was occupied with taking care of him and the boys. I don't remember them visiting me at all, although I suppose that can't be true.

Feel, her mother said, taking Susan's fingers and placing them behind her ear. The ridge of bone felt thin and flat, the skin a little puckered, although Susan couldn't make out a scar. The whole time that I was in the hospital, her mother said, no one ever combed or washed my hair. When I got out, my hair was so snarled and matted that my mother had to cut it off. My father screamed at her that I was ugly now. It was a long time before my hair grew back.

Susan leaned forward, stretched her arms out for a hug. She pressed her face against her mother's chest. She wanted to hug the little girl buried inside her mother now. She wanted to say, Don't leave.

Layla tov, my sweet, her mother said. Go to sleep.

If James hadn't gotten sick, Susan thinks now, probably she never would have seen him again. She lies back against her pillows and stares into the dark. She has finished her book but still can't fall asleep. She's sorry the story is over; she had wanted to read slowly, but found herself rushing, in spite of her intention, to the end. The blinds are open to the glow of the night sky. Her own reflection wavers, like a phantom, in the glass.

It was in 1995, a couple of years after James and Nicole had moved back to Australia, that she ran into Patrick at the airport, getting off the shuttle from D.C. Haven't you heard? he said. They stopped along the ramp by the racks of free magazines. Travelers hurried past as he shouted over the noise of the flight announcements crackling overhead. James had been diagnosed several months before. Some form of cancer; Patrick didn't know the details. The doctors had given him a 40 percent chance to live. He was in chemotherapy now. Yes, he was only thirty-three.

When she got back to the newsroom, she sat down right away and wrote James a note. How could she not have gotten back in touch? He was dying, for all she knew.

Two blocks away, the top-floor brownstone light snaps on. Susan squints, but the exhibitionist is nowhere to be seen. There is just the empty armchair, the bookshelf, the potted palm or fern. A yellow rectangle floating in the dark.

They all had lunch together a few months later, Susan and James and Nicole. He was in New York on business; Nicole was tagging along. It was the first and only time she met Nicole face-to-face. Up close, she was not as beautiful as Susan had supposed, although her eyes were a clearer blue and more intelligent than she'd wanted to believe. She had the kind of changeable face that could be made up to look elegant as a model's or scrubbed until all you noticed were the bare rims of her eyes, pink as a rabbit's. Good bones, Susan's mother would have said. Nicole was sitting at a table by herself, wearing an azure coat. James was late. She greeted Susan warmly and they clinked glasses of wine. She had the confident air, Susan thought, of a woman who had got her man. Despite the circumstances, she radiated calm.

Susan had readied herself for the worst, but James hadn't changed at all. He still had his energy and even all his hair. The latest test results were very good. The tumors were completely gone. If you had to get cancer, he joked, this was the one to get. Nicole smiled and reached out to take his hand. James kept his eyes on Susan as she did. But as usual, she misread the signs.

The light in the brownstone is still on, but the exhibitionist has not appeared. Could this be a signal of some kind? Susan reaches to turn off the bedside lamp, then changes her mind and dims it instead. She pulls off her own nightgown, leans back, slides her hand between her thighs.

It was a day or two after that lunch that she ran into James in the lobby of her building, as if by chance. That night he took her to a restaurant downtown. Over a bottle of wine, he told her the whole story of his illness—the meditation techniques he'd used to harness the healing energy of his mind; how, on what he'd imagined was his deathbed, a vision of her had suddenly appeared.

Me? Susan said.

Tears slid down his cheeks as he leaned forward across the table to take her hands. He clutched them so tightly she could feel her bones shift against his. Yes you, he said. His eyes were bright and blue. I had to see you again, he said, to let you know the way I felt. I couldn't believe that you might never know how much you meant to me. When I got your letter, I knew it was a sign.

My mother was only thirty-seven when she died, Susan's mother said. My father tried to save her. It drove him crazy that when it mattered most, he failed.

Susan has a disjointed memory of her own mother standing at a window, circling a hand over her breast. Sunlight shone through the thin cotton of her nightgown, revealing the outline of her belly and thighs. I am already older than she was when she died, her

mother said. Susan's father said, Come on, Leah! You're strong as
an ox! Her mother made a face, but it was obvious she felt re-
lieved.

Susan never knows quite what to put on those doctor's forms
that ask for your family history. *Cancer, check*. By the time they
operated on Susan's grandmother, it was already too late. It had
metastasized, spread everywhere. *Melanoma? Breast?* Back then no
one knew how to read the warning signs.

Now Susan follows doctor's orders, inspects her skin for changes,
taps her fingertips in concentric circles around her breasts. She,
too, is already older than her grandmother was then.

Susan's father calls her on her cell phone. Her cousin Gavi, he says,
was four cars behind the bus that blew up in Jerusalem today. He'd
gone there for work and was heading back to Haifa when it happened, right in front of him. Too close, her father says, this
time.

Susan thinks about calling Gavi but can't decide what she would
say. She sends him an e-mail instead, but he does not reply. At a
distance, it's hard to tell what's going on. Perhaps the language
barrier is too great. Or perhaps he simply doesn't want to corre-
spond.

She hasn't seen much of Gavi in the years since his breakdown
and divorce, since Sharona got the flat and custody of their kid. He
was living with his parents again, she'd heard. He'd been in and out
of work and couldn't afford an apartment of his own. He'd left the
"group," her father said, but now he said he had no friends.

Susan has a fantasy in which she rescues Gavi from what she
thinks of as his house arrest, restores him to his life. She flies to

Israel, sets him up in a new flat, restores him to happiness with her love. He's perfectly fine! she declares.

But what does she really know?

Here is what I see, James said. They were in bed together and it was late. They met at Susan's apartment in those last days, on James's periodic business trips to New York, or in out-of-town hotels. We're at your parents' place, out on the balcony. It's a lovely summer night, very dark and still. We're looking out at the Hudson, just like that time when you took me to—what was that place called?—the place where Toscanini lived. Yes. Wave Hill. So we're looking out at the Hudson in the dark and then I turn and lift you up and we start making love. Yes, right there. Of course you could! I lift up your skirt and you wrap your legs around my waist. Like that. Very slow. Only what you can't see, because you're turned the other way, is that your parents have come home. No, just listen. They see us but they don't turn on the light. They just stand there in the dark, watching us. It's not disgusting! They're happy. They're happy for your happiness. Why can't you accept that? Well, maybe that's what you want to believe. Maybe *you're* the one who can't let go of being their little girl.

He rescued me, Susan's mother said. She turned and smiled down at Susan, her hair swinging forward around her face. She was sitting on the edge of the bed, the mattress tilting slightly beneath her weight. Susan pressed her toes against her mother's back. By the time I married your father my parents were both dead. The first time we met, he stared at me and said, You are the girl I'm going to marry. What a line! I fell for it anyway.

Susan loved this story of her parents falling in love at first sight. It was the only happy one her mother told.

Even so, her mother went on, I kept hearing my father's voice inside my head. Does he come from a good family? Is there a history of mental illness or disease? My father had crazy, old-world ideas. They're not like us, I heard him say. Those assimilated German Jews are practically goys. I hadn't met your father's parents yet—in those days one didn't just zip around the world like we do now. How did I know he was really who he claimed to be? my roommate warned. He could be making it all up.

Susan's mother sighed and looked away, out of the bedroom, toward the hallway light. But he wasn't making it up, Susan said. No, her mother said. I don't know what I would have done if I hadn't met him. He saved my life.

Still, Susan wasn't sure her parents ever really got along. You wouldn't have called them soul mates, anyway. All her life, Susan worried that one of them would leave, but, for whatever reason, neither one of them ever did.

I always knew I wouldn't die, James said. It was early in the morning and they had just finished having sex. The smell of their bodies rose from the rumpled sheets. James liked to start making love to her while she was still asleep. She would wake to his lips against her ear, his hands circling her breasts, his insistent hard-on against her thighs. Nicole won't let me touch her like that, James said resentfully. She has everything she wants. The kids, the house in Paddington, backrubs every night.

Through the window, Susan could see that the exhibitionist's blinds were drawn. His apartment seemed farther away in daylight than lit up in the dark. Susan thought of that photograph of Nicole lying prone on windblown sand. The ridgeline of her pelvic bones, the round curve of her breasts. Now Nicole had an unfaithful husband, two small kids. Susan thought she understood that withholding was a form of power, too. She wouldn't trade places with Nicole. No.

James reached for the alarm clock, then swung his feet out of bed and ran his fingers through his hair. I have to go, he said, it's late. She looked up at the spray of freckles across his shoulders, the broad line of his back. He wasn't really her type at all. Probably that was what made them so well matched. Because she didn't try to keep him, he kept coming back.

She listened to the sound of the shower turning on. She waited for James to come back to the bedroom, freshly showered, his hair still wet, dressed in his suit and tie, for him to bend and kiss her on the forehead like a child while she pretended to have fallen back to sleep. You are very loved, he'd whisper, his lips against her ear, as if love were something that could envelop you like air, as if the one who loved her might be someone other than himself. She reached to the night table for her book, but she wasn't in the mood to read. She thought about how Hebrew had no word for *fiction*. A novel was simply a *sippur*, a story. A form of narrative. The closest term for *fiction* was *bidayon*, from the word *b'daya*, a falsehood or a lie. You never could tell which parts of stories people had made up, Susan knew. People told you what they needed to believe.

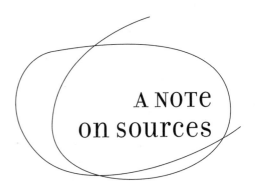

A NOTE
on sources

In this work of fiction, I have drawn on and transformed a range of factual materials in an effort to render the historical, political, and intellectual context of these stories as accurately as possible. For the history of the founding of the state of Israel and the Arab-Israeli conflict, I relied on many sources, notably *The Birth of the Palestinian Refugee Problem, 1947–1949* by Benny Morris and *Arab and Jew* by David Shipler. For information on biblical archeology, I depended on *The Bible Unearthed* by Israel Finkelstein and Neil Asher Silberman, *Hazor* by Yigael Yadin, articles about the Hazor excavations by Amnon Ben-Tor and Maria-Teresa Rubiato in the *Biblical Archaeology Review*, and the series of excavation reports on Hazor by Yigael Yadin, Amnon Ben-Tor, and others. Also essential was coverage of the Palestinian-Israeli conflict in *Ha'aretz*, *Commentary*, the *New York Times*, the *New York Daily News*, and elsewhere.